D0629350

What I
have
written

*What I
have
written*

A
NOVEL

JOHN A. SCOTT

W · W · NORTON & COMPANY

NEW YORK · LONDON

This book contains brief excerpts (often used slightly differently) from the
following works:

James Salter, *A Sport and a Pastime*. London: Jonathan Cape Ltd., 1985.
Jean-Paul Sartre, *Words* (trans. Irene Clephane). London: Penguin, 1967.
Harry Mathews, *Autobiography* and *Singular Pleasures* (from *The Way Home:
Collected Longer Poems*). London: Atlas Press, 1989.
Anaïs Nin, *The Diary of Anaïs Nin*. London: Peter Owen Publishers, 1967.

Manufacturing by The Haddon Craftsmen, Inc.

ISBN 0-393-03683-9

W. W. Norton & Company, Inc., 500 Fifth Avenue, New York, N.Y. 10110
W. W. Norton & Company Ltd., 10 Coptic Street, London WC1A 1PU

2 3 4 5 6 7 8 9 0

*Between one book and the next, there is the
empty space of a missing book, linked with we do
not know which of the two. We shall call it*
The Book of Torment, *appertaining to both.*

Edmond Jabès, The Book of Shares

CONTENTS

✤

CHRISTOPHER HOUGHTON

PARIS

✳ 1 ✳

Thursday, May 10. The day of Sainte
Solange. We have brought our illness to this town of the ill. To this
place of the aged and the dying.
Châtel-Guyon. Its central park, the
streets that curve downwards to
it – dark rivers to their lake –
flanked with elaborate hotels. These
edifices, white, ornate, with their
staunch bourgeois facades: Hôtel
Bellevue, Hôtel Splendide, Hôtel
Grande . . . From another place,

Belvedere, Ritz. American, this town of hotels.

Bleak foyer: an extrusion of light, glim, the colour of vegetable stock.

'*One* night?' the girl is asking in English – even though our conversation has to this point taken place in French – turning the large white pages of the register. It is usual to stay for one of the prescribed periods. She is shaking her head. We are clearly here by mistake if we wish just the single night. I smile: ours is, of course, a more subtle malady.

I watch her hand move down the columns of names and dates. The skin has a darkness typical of the Auvergne. Her wrists are thick, the cuffs of her white blouse pulled tight. I see where the material has creased, the lines converging at the button in rills.

Behind the desk, which extends in a narrow semicircle from the wall, a doberman paces back and

4

forth. It rears suddenly, dabbing the counter with its paws, then slides, failing to gain traction on the smooth surface, nails clicking against the marble. It returns to the floor and sighs: an exhalation of impatience.

'Ah, yes,' says the girl in English, looking up from the register, 'it is possible.'

I catch a glimpse of Gillian moving through the entrance. The whiteness of her face seems to have dislodged, its pallor smeared across the tainted air like a vapour trail.

The elevator is small – our two suitcases occupy more than half the floor space – its ascent excruciatingly slow. An arrow arcing from *RDC* to *4* on the half-clockface above the door is the only indication of movement. Pasted to the back wall is a notice requesting the cessation of all noise at 21.00h.

I go, as usual, to the windows. I look out across this small provincial town. Below, the streets meander in their steepnesses, the cobble washed by shadow from the buildings. It is 4.15, but dusk seems already upon us. To the right the view is dominated by a hill: at its summit the body of Christ, His arms outspread upon a cross of neon.

I turn to the room. I see Gillian entering the *salle de bains*. On the wall above the double bed is a list of doctors and their after-hours numbers in event of an emergency. The main table is strewn with leaflets: advertisements for periodic treatments, testimonials to the efficacy of the magnesium cure. Beside the leaflets, as if a part of this profusion, is a *Paris Match* of some five months before. On its cover are the statues of Versailles, swathed in canvas to protect them from the acid rain and from the cold of winter which never came.

We eat at the hotel restaurant. Everything is *à l'Anglais*: tepid pulps of varying flavour, suited to the toothless.

The dining-room is full. At every table but ours, the medication pouches have been set alongside the cutlery. Those who are permitted have poured themselves a single glass of wine. The recorked bottles – each bearing its owner's name – dot the tablecloths.

Gillian and I eat in silence. We have not spoken now for three weeks – the odd sentence, certainly, but silence has secured itself. To end it now would be unthinkable. What could this first conversation possibly be? What words could carry such significance?

To break this monotony, especially in the long periods of the car journey, I conduct mock dialogues with myself: speeches so quiet that, should they provoke enquiry, I could reasonably deny their utterance. Of course, we speak where it is necessary in the presence of others – amongst those we have met, or with the occasional visitor from home. And we order meals. At Sarlat, only yesterday, I ordered fresh asparagus; I ordered rabbit with a mustard sauce, with beans and spinach; I ordered a *bleu d'Auvergne*, a *Rigotte de Pelussin* and a *Cantalon*. A bottle of 1984 Bordeaux.

And perhaps it is simply that her look is held too long, or else it is the half-glance back – the briefest hint of indecision, a wish for the implausible. I note the straight dark French hair, the starch of the white cap and apron, the black dress, the stocking seams, the black patent leather of the shoes.

It is as if Gillian, by her simple presence, were the sole barrier to the possession of this woman; as though the possibility of these liaisons is predicated upon her absence.

It is resentment then, at what she has continued to deny me, that characterises my feelings first of all. This is the source of my hatred.

As it is, I can say nothing to this young woman. She brings the bill on a white saucer and thanks me. I stare at her writing, aroused by the overwhelming childishness of her hand. Its innocence. I extrapolate the necessary pallor of her nipples from this script, the belly's flatness, the sparse, fine, cat-hair of her sex. I wish to ejaculate across the bill – to see the ink dissolve, the paper darken.

The *salle de bains* is separated from the main room by an elaborate timber partition into which a plastic concertina door has been placed. I pull across this door and secure the tiny metal latch. I watch myself slowly unbuttoning the shirt. I loosen the cord of the trousers. I step out of these pooled materials.

I slide off my underpants, pushing them down with my hands pressed tight to my thighs. I turn both taps full on and enter the shower. I remove the rose and its coiled metal tube from the hook. I direct the water, needle-fine, underneath the shaft of my penis – moving it full-length back and forth from the testicles to the glans. The head is bobbing on the jet of water, the fine spray flying at my face, blinding me. I feel the semen rising. I redirect the spray only at the last second. The penis spasms, but there is no ejaculation. Only the appearance of the smallest pearl of fluid at the eye. Opaque. A clouded tear. As if it had wept for me. Again I direct the spray against the glans. This time, however, I take the flannel, cramming it inside my mouth to prevent my cries. The taste is bitter. I watch the semen fall, undissolved amidst the water. I watch it cling against the grill of the drain. I crush the tiny snakes of fluid with my heel, sliding my foot back and forth across the metal. It is gone.

Perhaps Gillian believes this place will cure us: otherwise why should she reach to me in this bed made for the dying, her hand coming to rest low on my belly, her fingertips touching the edge of my hair. It is significant she has chosen this night, within minutes of my self-relief, when all desire has drained from me.

Already I have invented this convenient fiction that her touch seeks my attention only – and not my arousal.

'Is something the matter?' I enquire.

She turns from me, towards the darkness. Possibly she cries. If not this night, then another.

I awake just before dawn. I slide from the bed, moving with the unsteadiness of those recently awoken.

From the window I watch the fallen angels shuddering across the basin of this valley, their wings tinted by the light of the neon cross. They are scouring the streets for souls. In this darkest hour – I am not familiar with the French equivalent of our proverb – they collect the frailest from this town of hotels. I detect one peering at me from a distance of some fifty metres. He raises his cap. I smile and shake my head.

Three rooms away, Madame F—— from Strasbourg reaches for the telephone, but the hand has never moved. She finds that she is watching her own motionless arm – fallen outside the sheets, a diagonal across her bulbous form (still in bed beside her sleeping husband) – from outside the window.

'*Allez! Allez!*' cry the angels, and she is gone. Without the opportunity to pack. Wearing only this nightdress. Thank God, she thinks, it is a temperate night . . .

It would be easier to suppose I have been dreaming, but I find that I am truly at the window staring at the very first of light and these creatures moving off into the distance as if they were returning night-birds.

In the morning nothing is said. We arise and prepare to view the town. We walk to the Centre Thermal and the park. There is a dolorous alacrity to our movements.

From the foyers of the hotels comes a steady stream, glacial in its pace: the aged are moving down the stairs from their night's rest. It is *l'heure du verre d'eau* – their time to drink at the springs. Everyone is carrying a small cup, a bag for the various medications, and a towel.

We stand before the Source Gubler VI dite Carnot, the air perpetually sour with magnesium. The aged push us aside, barging with a skeletal vigour. '*Pardon!*'

they demand, and move to the long curved bench named Marguerite, gabbling in their various dialects.

The bells above the main pavilion are ringing. A summoning of the faithful. But there are no messiahs here to greet them. Instead there are bronzed masseurs and sports leaders. There are nurses: dark, thick-wristed girls of the Auvergne.

The entrance foyer is dominated by information booths and cashiers: to the left for women, to the right for men. Gillian and I depart on our separate inspections.

I go no further than the pool. Its edges are festooned with the dying: mouths fallen open, vacant-eyed. The colonel from Versailles, the cold dough of his shoulders marbled with stretchmarks; the banker from Toulouse, his chest a darkened scouring-board. They are both here – putting lie to the benign surrender – the raw and the cooked.

Late Friday, afternoon or evening. A viewless corner room, upstairs in the Hôtel Moderne. The roofs of Autun. Diagonals of tile, dark with moss. It is as *A Sport and a Pastime* has described it, though not as I had imagined from that description.

'None of this is true,' the book says, halfway down page seventeen. 'I've said Autun, but it could easily have been Auxerre. I'm sure you'll come to realise that.'

But this is Autun. I remember the description: 'The amphitheatre. The great, central square: the Champ de Mars.' I have chosen this place by way of homage. By way of remembering.

A month before. Maundy Thursday. James Salter, returning again to Paris from the States, gives a reading at the Village Voice Bookshop, rue Princesse, in the sixth *arrondissement*. It is held upstairs, in the area devoted to history and psychology. Seven o'clock on a hot, airless

Parisian evening, the space crowded with anglophones: Americans, of course, and then the British. And Australians.

I recognise Clare Murnane; there is a space for me to stand beside her chair.

'Avery!' she cries, and gestures with her free hand – the cigarette now at her lips. 'There's room over here!' Her words roll out in smoke above the audience.

'Avery,' she says, as I approach, 'where *have* you been? We've been waiting for your call . . . ' She stops. 'You won't know Catherine.'

And so it is I meet her eyes, and everything that I shall tell begins. This red-haired woman, Catherine Danon, who might possibly be forty-seven, who might reasonably be some ten years older than myself.

Salter, accompanied by a woman in a greyish suit, makes his appearance at the top of the staircase. The two pick their way through the ragged obstacles of chairs. Clare is enquiring after Gillian, expressing a certain interested surprise at her absence. I offer some reply.

'Oh, I see,' she says. 'I *do* see, don't I?'

'Yes,' I say, above the sudden outbreak of applause. I return to Catherine, to find that I have met her eyes again. Nor is there any movement on her part to shift them from me.

There is a brief introduction by the woman, who, we find, is on the editorial staff of *The Paris Review*. Salter seems much younger than his sixty-four years. He holds himself straight-backed, his body 'well kept'. And with the moustache, there is an almost military presence to the man.

He reads a short story, 'Foreign Shores', from *Dusk*, his latest work: a young girl named Truus, an exchange of pornographic letters.

We have chosen the brasserie in rue du Four, across from the Mabillon entrance. I confess (of course with reservations: in particular the beggars and the staleness of the air) my fondness for the Metro.

'The Metro!' Clare exclaims. 'I haven't used the Metro now for over seven years.' She lights a cigarette. 'I walk,' she says, 'or, if it's late, I take a cab.'

I lift the copy of *A Sport and a Pastime* from the table. It is a book I first discovered in the early seventies. After the reading I had asked Salter for his signature, indicating my great admiration for the work. He had written his name, nothing else. He seemed uninterested in my enthusiasms.

I find myself staring at the signature, scrawled between his printed name and the title: the 'J' broken from 'ames', the unjoined bar hovering above the hook.

I talk about the opening descriptions – the evocation of a French landscape I have yet to see. I talk about the dreadful longing of the narrator in the face of Dean and Anne-Marie's affair.

'The opening is wonderful, of course,' says Catherine. 'I seem to spend half my time in French trains watching those little stations . . . ' She smiles as if in memory and then the smile has died. 'But ultimately, it disappointed me. I found their lovemaking repetitive, without imagination. And Anne-Marie is so uninteresting. I'm always irritated by men who find a girl exciting because she says '*oui*' instead of 'yes.' She pauses. 'You are in Paris for long?'

Until late May. Six weeks. But then next Tuesday I am leaving for the provinces – the Loire Valley, the Perigord, the Auvergne – and will be gone a month.

'And you are travelling alone?' she asks.

I watch as Catherine turns towards the street outside. An old woman is threading her way, apologetically, down rue du Four: her body is quite crippled, bent forward from the waist, as if at any moment she might stop to retrieve an object from the pavement.

I return my gaze to Catherine. The corner of her mouth betrays a trace of anxiety, a hesitancy, before she brings herself to sip the coffee from the demitasse.

'What are you working on these days?' asks Clare.

I talk about the second book of poems. I see that Catherine has turned, her eyes direct and close to mine, as if, were we alone, she would be offering her sex to me.

'I would love to read it, Avery,' she says. 'Is this possible?'

I tell her that I have some finished sections back at the apartment. Perhaps if she would give me her address I could send a copy through the mail before I leave.

She rises from the table, moving to the counter of the brasserie. There is a small display of postcards. She chooses one, without offering any payment, and brings it to the table. I watch the trace of her handwriting across the card. Clare is examining the bill and reaching in her bag.

'Now, I must have you both to dinner as soon as you return,' she says, fastening the clip, placing a fifty-franc note, a ten-franc coin in the saucer. 'You've been very selfish, Avery, not having got in touch sooner. We're all very much in debt to Mr. Salter!'

I glance at Catherine, the fineness of her bones: the collarbone, the neck. The dark red – auburn – of her hair.

'And now we must be off. Or Claude will fret. Are you right, Catherine?'

She offers me the postcard. It is

an advertisement, now some two weeks out of date, for the tenth *Salon du Livre*, at the Grand Palais: *Le Livre au coeur de la réussite*. On the reverse she has written the name of a street in the fifth *arrondissement*.

'So, you have my address,' she says.

My only thought now, to return to the apartment, to lock the bathroom door and bring myself to a release; so urgent this need, that even our farewells become unbearably prolonged.

We wait perhaps three minutes more, then we too are compelled to follow all the other patrons from the restaurant onto the street.

The accident has involved a motor cyclist and a Mercedes sports. Perhaps five minutes has elapsed, but already only the aftermath remains: the car, mounted high on the footpath; the crumpled motor cycle; oil, blood.

'*Qu'est-ce qui s'est passé?*' I ask.

Of course, the scene has changed: she is no longer with me; these are not the streets of Paris. We are back here, in Autun. The man begins his explanation. His French has the typical slowness of the region. It is not difficult to understand the substance. It is a bad corner. What has happened is nothing exceptional. Most of the onlookers are there solely to make comparisons – it has almost become obligatory. I turn back to find Gillian staring at the blood. She is astride it, as if the flow were hers.

It is morning. The Cathédrale Saint-Lazare. Dankness. The chlorine trace of stone. My gaze is turned upward to these figures carved some seven hundred years ago.

A demon pushes a young couple into a vast urn. Whole cities have preceded them. There! A tower disappears into the opening. Everything re-emerges in Hell. I recognise Madame F— from the hotel at Châtel-Guyon. She has been forced to shed her nightdress. This then is the destination of those flying souls – as most certainly it is ours. Here everyone is naked as if prepared for sex. Here everyone – even the most beautiful – has been transformed: remade in their inner uglinesses as the Church has warned would come to pass.

Gillian waits beneath a stone statue. Our paths have rejoined here, significantly. Perhaps she has been praying. I look for the trace of blood at her lips, for the smear of blood on the back of her hands where she has attempted to wipe it free.

The hair of the figure above us has been sculpted in small bulbs the size of profiteroles: a tree of buds. The nose is flattened, the mouth stretched sideways not unlike the opening of a letterbox. It is crouched in the posture of a cringing dog: *Diable du Désespoir. The Devil of Despair.*

We move out into a sunlight we could not have believed to still exist. The weather has been unseasonably temperate for these four weeks. We have seen clouds amassing, only to move off in an opposite direction as if in fear of us.

For our return to Paris, once again we drive into clear weather.

※ 2 ※

The freeways are impossible. At every point of merging, the traffic seizes. Back and forth one passes the same cars, is passed; edging in the lanes, back and forth. The temperature gauge climbs; the automatic fan begins to hum. I unfold the map, considering another *porte*. It is impossible. In any case, a decision has already been made. When in doubt, say no. At last, a French proverb.

We move slowly beyond *la périphé-rique*. This city marked on its borders by these towers arisen from lots razed like bombsites. This city of small cities. Each *arrondissement* with its own heart. City of spheres. City of these dark, straight-haired women.

The air is mauve with exhaust, incubated by the coming summer. Still. Tinted. As though the skins of grapes had been added to the light. *L'air taché*. Mauve air studded with the yellow globes of approaching headlights. A flood of warnings.

Perhaps ultimately it is these streets: the narrowness of their *ruelles*, the grandeur of their boulevards. Plethora: streets in their densities, threading together in hair or handwriting. Is it possible to miss this place as one might a woman, or a woman as this place?

It is dark at our return. Too late to buy food. No, that is not true: the Algerian shop in rue Saint Antoine will be open. We are too exhausted for the necessary preparations. Instead we visit La Maroc. We order *couscous royale* and a *pichet* of red wine.

Across from us there sits an English couple. They have little French. The owner is telling them he will look after everything. He invites them to the rear of the restaurant where the entrées are extravagantly displayed on a large table.

'You must help yourselves,' he is saying. 'Everything is delicious. Fresh.'

'What are those?' the English wife is asking.

'Delicious!' he replies.

We watch their return. Their

plates crammed with Moroccan delicacies. A waiter brings the 'house' wine: an imported Moroccan red. In this restaurant no menus are provided. The owner will look after everything.

Now a couscous is brought to their table. Already they have eaten too much. Now they begin to argue. They blame each other for allowing all this food to arrive. They cannot bring themselves to send it back, or to stop a further course from arriving.

Several young Moroccan girls have gathered at the front bar. Their dresses are gaudy and tight, the cheap fabrics glistening. It is a Saturday evening. The room is full with 'family'. Their men are already playing cards at an end table. Occasionally they call to each other the length of the restaurant.

For the English couple, nothing can now be disputed. They are surrounded by the enemy. The untouched couscous is removed and replaced by another dish.

The table nearest the exit is occupied by a drunkard, in his fifties, wrapped in a grey gaberdine overcoat. He is unshaven. Not quite a *clochard*. He calls to the young Moroccan girls. One answers him: a single word, and there is general laughter.

A cat has approached the table of the English couple. It rubs its body against the legs of the wife. I watch her bend, pick up the animal and enfold it in her arms.

Like us, the couple have been reduced to silence. It is as if their table had been replaced by a mirror. I lift the wineglass to my mouth expecting to see the husband's glass similarly rise.

He has requested *l'addition*. The house red has been billed at a hundred francs. I witness their evident despair. They barely have enough money to pay. She is hunting through her bag for coins.

The couple move from the

table – now occupied only by the stretching cat, inclining itself towards the food on the oilcloth. The drunkard watches their exit. Momentarily he glances back to their table, still brim with the third, untouched, course. I see him suddenly stand in agitation, shouting with concern after the couple.

'*Madame! Vous avez oublié votre chat!*'

A sudden change in weather. Late spring brings an undecided rain: intermittent. Skies sullen. Overcast. The clouds move eastward – increasingly dark – running against the movement of the Seine, directly in my line of vision. It seems, if I do not focus, that the darkness slides down the face of the window.

On the streets everything is impregnated with a sense of decay. The cardboard cartons across the metal bars of the grills have returned, along with the abandoned bottles of the *clochards*.

The reflection of a tree branch in the sloping back window of a car gives the appearance of shattered glass.

Another day. At this same window. A building sign: *Pierre de taille. Marbrerie. Maçonnerie. Béton armé.* A row of terraces at the end of our street has disappeared behind sheets of corrugated fibreglass. I listen to the endless chipping at the old facades: the Algerian workers on the scaffolding, their uniforms – caps and workclothes – like convicts. Bottles of Evian on the wooden planks. Plastic sheeting flapping loudly in the wind. At times a bellow. On the turret roofs of the fourth floor, the pigeons, heads down, puffed up in their aggression, turn in ever-advancing circles.

Behind me I can hear the scratching of Gillian's pen. She is writing in her Paris Journal – her book of days. Now from the bedroom I hear her voice ascending in its constant scales. I call, enquiring if she intends to be much longer.

It is our seventh year together. This is significant, perhaps. But I believe it to be mere coincidence. What has happened and is happening could have happened three and four and, yes, I will say it, even seven years ago.

We have received the dinner invitation from Clare Murnane and her husband, Claude. It is for May 24, Ascension, a public holiday. We are to dine with the American novelist Harry Mathews and his partner, Marie Chaix. Catherine Danon has also been invited, but she is still finishing her work in Brussels: she will join the party later, possibly for coffee.

I have come to know these occasions. Dinner conversations that lapse suddenly and inexplicably into French, as if the city were asserting itself. As if it could abide this travesty of foreignness no longer.

So it is that Gillian and I are to be a couple once more, these several hours. Always with me, this ghost presence at the periphery of my vision, her voice in its depleted counterpoint like the cry of a baby from a distant room – how can this be possible? And then I realise how easy it might be to continue like performers in an exquisite piece of theatre, genteel, urbane: meeting the American novelist, the French biographer; making conversation; carrying a bottle of Saumur, *méthode champenoise*, itself an adequate impersonation.

It is of course not possible. We are betrayed at every moment. And to-night, particularly, it is crucial that I play a double game: so everyone will understand our act to *be* an act.

The nearest Metro is La Muette
in the sixteenth *arrondissement*.
We make a *correspondance* at
Opéra, the sound of African drums
drifting to us from a connecting
tunnel, like a blood. At the entrance to the platform we hear the
roar of an incoming train. We begin
to run. The rush of stale air –
warm, used, stinking of elec-
tricity – hits my face. The siren
sounds; the doors hiss shut
behind us. This time the compartment is reasonably uncrowded.
Gillian takes a seat by the opposite
door – drawing the hem of her
coat free from the floor as she sits.
I slide my ticket beneath my watch-
band and take hold of the stainless-
steel upright. The transfer on the
window adjacent to the central
seats – those reserved AUX MUTILÉS
DE GUERRE – has been predictably
altered. The last three letters of
GUERRE have been scratched away,
the first three meticulously
amended to CUL. For those

wounded in the arse.

I stare at the impassive faces of the passengers, silent in the warm and stale electric air.

At Pompe an Algerian woman, a baby held beneath one arm, enters the carriage. In her other hand she holds a square of white cardboard on which are several sentences printed in childish capitals with a black felt pen. Without speaking, the woman moves amongst the passengers, holding the card close to their faces. A few have offered two-franc pieces. She accepts them without comment, without thanks, and moves to the next person.

I stare at the card. It appears to be a brief biography, though I do not have time to read beyond the first sentence. It is a simple variation of the stories chalked by the beggars in the Metro tunnels: those who do not ever meet your eyes, those for whom what is written is the only speech. I wonder if this story is true. Whether the elaborateness of the tale is an indication of desperation or deceit. Possibly I fail to give her money because I doubt the authenticity of a confession I cannot follow.

The train pulls in to La Muette. The woman and her child move out with us, only to reboard the train a carriage down.

I find myself standing opposite a poster for a current film: a floating cherub with the erection of a fullgrown man.

Mathews and Marie Chaix arrive. He appears as in the photographs on the covers of his books, but without the cigarette.

Clare makes the necessary introductions in English. Claude, her husband, exchanges greetings in French. Catherine, Clare mentions again for their benefit, may be joining them later – perhaps for coffee. I note how doubt has crept into her explanation. The possibility of her absence sickens me: the evening has been rendered pointless.

As Mathews sits on the couch, he asks if he may have one of Clare's cigarettes. So now the portrait is complete. I watch him light it, savour the first inhalation, hold it out before him as if it were the stem of a wineglass.

Jean-Paul – a precocious long-haired child, somewhere between seven and nine years old – has a chapter ready from his latest novel to show Monsieur Mathews. It is called *Pour un Papillon*. It is enscribed in an exercise book in violet ink.

A scientist and his daughter are clinging to a buoy, calling to each other.

' "Daisy!" '

' "Papa!" '

As they call, a shark approaches.

' "Sharks are common in the

tropical Atlantic. These large and voracious saltwater fish may be as much as forty feet long and weigh up to eight tons." '

Mathews has provided the translation for us.

'It's not a scientist,' says Jean-Paul. 'It's a butterfly collector.' Adding with ironic resignation, '*Mais ça ne fait rien.*'

He retrieves his exercise book and leaves the room: '*Je sais fort bien que je ne suis qu'une machine à faire des livres!*'

As if filling the space left by his departure, in the doorway stands a girl of sixteen. She bears a strong physical resemblance to her mother: the same blue eyes shadowed by dark lashes, the same pallor of complexion. It was her whiteness that loomed first against the hall's dark background. Her body is exquisite. She wears a high skirt to emphasise the stilt-like legs. At her breasts I notice an apparent discolouration of the material: a swollen darkness of the areola uncommon in her age. I imagine her pregnant.

'This is Adèle,' says Clare. 'My daughter.' She is off to a dance.

There is an episode in Mathews's book *Singular Pleasures* which I find particularly moving. It is the incident in the Barcelona brothel where the 27-year-old man masturbates whilst watching an older woman undress. She is the absolute embodiment of his fantasies. She calls for him to wait, but he doesn't want to wait – he wants above all to see the real her undress, as he so often has seen her do in his fantasies. But she is too quick for him. She moves to him swiftly, sits astride him, her stockinged thighs across him. He comes inside her. He feels... a blackness? I try to remember the phrase.

' "... something beyond pleasure, regret, desire... " ' Mathews finishes the extract from memory. ' "A flashing blackness that leaves him unconscious as she, with a compassionate laugh, gathers him in her arms!" '

We sit around the dining table as at a seance.

'My father,' says Marie Chaix, 'was a fascist. A member of the Parti Populaire Français. I wrote his story in a novel. In English it was called *The Laurels of Lake Constance* – perhaps you know of it? It was how I came to meet Harry.'

Mathews continues. It is a history he has recounted before. It is now part of the grand myth of their relationship.

'I'd been offered the job of translating Marie's novel whilst I was visiting New York in 1975. At that stage I'd never heard of the book, though it'd been a bestseller in France. I agreed because I'd assumed it'd be an easier task than the avant-garde stuff I'd previously been working on. Of course, it ended up being harder and much more affecting than I'd expected. In fact, it quite overwhelmed me.

'I remember writing to Marie from Venice. The book had a rather discreetly alluring photograph on the cover. I was hoping it might prove more than an ordinary acquaintance.' He smiles and takes the time to ash the cigarette. 'I used every writer's trick I knew to make myself sound interesting – and when I'd finished the letter I tore it up! I thought the authoress deserved a little better than my disguised come-on. So I wrote again, a new letter, short, courteous, respectful . . . '

'At the time I was a resolutely devoted spouse and a mother of two,' adds Marie Chaix. 'I almost left my family to pay Mr Mathews a visit in Venice.'

'It was as if that first letter had been encrypted in the second. Six weeks later we had our first phone conversation, mostly about the book, but over that hour something happened – not entirely in my imagination, because when we met two weeks later it was clear that something new, something quite 'impossible', had come into our lives.' He pauses. 'We've never left each other since.'

I find myself saying, 'Bravo.' Claude smiles benignly on the couple and, no doubt seduced by the general glow, drinks their health.

Clare has entered the room with a large casserole, which she places in the centre of the table. She lifts the lid: *Gibelotte de lapin*. The air is suffused with the ingredients of the fricassee: the rabbit, the bacon, the Dijon mustard, the mushrooms and the baby onions, the white wine and veal stock . . .

'I found Jean-Paul still scribbling away at Claude's desk,' she announces. 'I told him it was getting very dark and he'd ruin his eyes, and he said, "*Même dans le noir je pourrais écrire!*" "I can write even in the dark!" ' she translates for us, and laughs. I notice her gums have been bleeding from too many cigarettes.

I have gone in search of the WC. I wish to hear the conversation continue beyond me – to be freed from the necessity of keeping it alive, to diminish it with my distance – the rise of voices, the occasional laughter breaking like a sea against its shore.

The apartment is serviced by a narrow corridor (two people would, if meeting there, need to turn side-on, or move back into the doorway of an adjoining room) running from the entrance and making two ninety-degree turns to the right. I make the second of these turns now. The passage ends at a slightly open door. I pause and then am drawn inside. I turn on the light. My eyes move straight away to the windows: have I become suddenly visible? The blind has been drawn. It is Adèle's room.

Near the door is an open-topped wicker basket used for soiled clothing. Beneath a damp towel – on top of a pair of American jeans, a T-shirt, a pair of small white underpants shrivelled together by the elastic – is a brassière: flesh-coloured, discarded.

I hear the 'clock' of footsteps that have broken from the distant conversation like a solo passage in some concerto: a woman's heels upon the polished boards of the apartment. The stride is confident, assured of the space, the distances.

The switch to Adèle's room flicks back with a loose metallic click. I enter the toilet, gently pushing to the door – the handle raised to avoid the sound of closing. I listen as the footsteps go past the entrance to the kitchen, pause as if the person were assuring themselves of something, checking on some detail, then move back to the kitchen.

I hear the taxi pull up below. Of course it could be any car that has arrived. Only the time – it is shortly before 11.00 – increases the likelihood. But if it had happened at 9.00, I would have had the same sense of expectation. I know the moment of her arrival. I sense her very presence in the street.

With the exception of Clare, the others continue in their conversations, oblivious. In such a city it would be lunatic to pause at every arriving car. I watch Clare move to the window and look down. I imagine her staring at the foreshortened players, the roof of the taxi, the bonnet, the person who sits just inside the door, her legs already swung out to the footpath, searching for the fare.

'Claude!' she cries, but also

glances momentarily to me, '*Voilà*, Catherine!'

We share a taxi home, the three. Catherine talks at some length with the driver. There is a disagreement about which apartment should be driven to first. We swing by the Metro at Alma and have joined the Cours Albert Premier, travelling eastwards along the banks of the Seine, part of an advancing yellow-lighted mass on the unlaned boulevard.

We have stopped outside our apartment. Catherine is writing her address on the back of a bookmark. She passes it to Gillian: this address I have repeated to myself a thousand times! She is insisting that we come for lunch tomorrow – it is perfect, she will be free all day.

Gillian reminds me that to-morrow is the day of Godfrey's

return from England. There are preparations to be made. He is expecting us to meet him at the airport that same afternoon. She pauses. Her refusal has been embarrassing, overlaid with too much excuse. Perhaps it would be possible for me to go alone? Would Catherine be offended if she remained at our apartment? Of course not. I agree. We are to meet at 1.00. No, earlier if you must get away. At 12.30.

So Gillian has sealed this. Everything has happened.

I hear the treble of the taxi radio scratching messages across our arrangements. The driver seems impatient with this hurried outbreak of English, these foreigners crammed into the back seat of his vehicle.

Gillian presses fifty francs insistently into Catherine's hand for our part of the journey. It is ridiculous, says Catherine. Another minute passes.

I watch the departing taxi, hear its tyres slapping on the irregular cobblestones.

Throughout the evening, Catherine has barely spoken to me. Above all else, she has made no mention of my poems. She has carried on this first duplicity with the absolute discretion of a whore.

Inside the apartment I pour a glass of La Limousine I purchased at Les Eyzies, its colour a garish green. From next door I hear the sound of Miles Davis's *Kind of Blue*: the piano solo from 'Freddy Free-loader'.

I retire to the toilet. I take the folded brassière from my pocket. I gently run my fingers across the inside of the loose cups where Adèle's nipples would have pressed. I remain convinced that without this talisman Catherine would not have arrived. That my planned unfaith-fulness had manifested her. That she had come to claim me with a far stronger desire.

Friday, May 25. The day of Sainte Sophie. On my right I pass rue Grenier-sur-l'Eau. Blocked to traffic by large concrete bollards, it has become a makeshift handball court for the adjoining public school. The furthest footpath seems perpetually littered with the excrement of dogs.

Each evening on my walk I have watched these animals: squatting, staring glazedly ahead as if preparing to lift some immense weight. Their bodies bear down. Again, and again. Now they are running. Exuberant. Released from their dreadful burdens. They are delivered souls. They are weightless. They float off into the darkening air.

Twelve fifteen. A row of schoolgirls sit, their backs leaning against the bars of the Jewish Memorial. In the masonry it is still possible to see the bullet holes from the terrorist attack. They have become another part of the memorial. Nothing here will be forgotten. The legs of the girls are drawn up close to their chests. The brown undersides of their thighs are visible, as are the soft white triangles of their knickers. Boys loiter in front of them, anxious for glimpses of their sex. They assume my nationality from my appearance. They use the word 'English' as I pass, and laugh.

We shall have two hours. To begin and to end. I have imagined this conversation, rehearsed it in every waking hour of the previous night. A sufficient thread of narrative – and no more – to allow the sexual act to plausibly commence. The plotline of a pornographic magazine.

She moves ahead of me. Her skin – a redhead's skin; darkly

freckled on the shoulders, the back – exposed by the white dress. It has two straps, each an inch wide. It is firmly drawn across the bust down to below the waist, where it flares out slightly.

We sit at opposite ends of the couch. Our bodies diagonalled. Backs wedged into the corners. Our legs almost touching in the space in front of the middle seat.

'The rents here are impossible,' she is saying. 'Another rise, and I shall have to move.' She brings a bottle of muscadet. I tell her how, since my trip to the provinces, it has become my favourite wine.

Her legs, only slightly marked by freckles, are unstockinged. It is quite possible that she is naked beneath this dress, the material of which neither confirms nor denies this.

'We are very much alike,' she says. 'I read your poems. They have a sadness to them which suggests some prior intimacy. Their language is that of the *petite mort*. They expose too much of you.' She pauses. 'Or maybe it's because I'm just coming to the end of an affair myself.'

The 'myself' seems to draw me into this situation. Incriminates me. It must be obvious – Gillian and I – our bodies must exude these desperations.

'It's very convenient. He lives in London. In our jobs we both have reasons to cross the channel frequently. We've been involved now for seven months and yet I know nothing about him. He tells me the English are very closed, and I say, 'Change.' And he agrees, of course, but there is nothing. The sex is very good, but I need to know the person – otherwise it's *just* the sex and it dies.' She reaches for her glass.

'I lived too long with a French-man – my husband – for seventeen years. He spoilt me. My next man must be very special. Very different.' The wine has reached her mouth as punctuation. Her eyes not leaving mine.

It is clear that I must also now reveal myself. Share some corresponding intimacy. I find myself confiding to her as I would to a friend of many years. I tell her of the final weeks with Gillian. It is my first betrayal. I offer up her suffering – this history rewritten – on the altar of my uninhibitedness.

'We do not speak together now, at all,' I tell her.

'How impossible it must be for you,' she says.

On the mantelpiece there are two photographs. My eyes have returned to them several times that afternoon. Now, in her momentary absence, I have moved to them.

Drawn by them.

Each is a portrait of a young woman: one in black and white, possibly dating from the late thirties or early forties, the other recent. I cannot help but notice the dark red, the auburn of the hair.

'My daughter.' Catherine stands close beside me. She takes the frame from my hands. I have no recollection of having picked it up from the shelf. 'Danielle.'

She stares a moment at the photograph. She has been captured by its history, that second. Into a meaning that might never be communicated to another.

'She will be twenty in September. It's hard to accept one's child as another woman. She would find it difficult too, possibly, to see *me* in the same way. As a woman with her needs, desires. Some weekends she stays here with her lover. It is strange – you hear the sound of their lovemaking . . . '

She replaces it beside the other

photograph.

'And my mother.' She pauses. 'I have lost them both.'

I tell her I was twenty-one before *my* first sexual encounter – still cowering beneath the shadow of a guilt, it seems to me now, quite self-imposed.

'One of my greatest diversions is initiating young men in sex,' she says. 'I have an artist friend in Australia, Marion Harpur. Perhaps you know her work? Her son was travelling through Europe – it was his first time away from home – and we arranged that he would spend a week with me in Paris.

'Late on his second night here, there was a knock on my bedroom door – I was in bed watching something on the television – could he watch the program too? Of course I agreed. I offered him a place beside me on the bed. He seemed quite painfully embarrassed at the suggestion and spent the evening with a cushion on the floor.

'The next two nights the same thing happened – only he would want to watch the programs later and later. It was impossible to sleep, even with the volume down. And then one night he simply came into my room and sat beside me. He was trembling. He told me he had wanted to make love to me from the very first night. We spent two weeks together. He wished to move into my apartment permanently. I remember when I told him it was impossible, he cried.'

The afternoon is gone. The time of parting has been predetermined. It cannot be changed. Gillian has made arrangements for us to meet Godfrey at the airport by 4.30.

We are to leave France in two days; our final moments will be filled with him: lunches, visits, sharing of stories. We will be obliged once again to act out a relationship under constant scrutiny.

I wonder if perhaps Catherine will invite me to remain for a final drink – but there is no insistence.

'It is a pity we didn't meet sooner,' she says. I agree. We are both standing.

'Goodbye, Avery,' she says, kissing the air to my left and to my right cheek. She moves back from her embrace, but our bodies are still touching, our arms still half retaining the other's body. We move into a deeper kiss. I can feel her hips and lower belly thrusting forward, the bone of her mound hard against my penis. My hands lift the weight of this auburn hair from her neck. Our mouths, still held slightly open, move apart. One cannot kiss again. There is only sex now, or this departure.

'I shall miss you, Avery,' I hear her say.

She does not wait in the doorway watching my departure. She returns to her apartment. She closes the door. Doubtless she moves to the table, takes the glass of muscadet and brings it to her mouth. Much of the coolness has gone. The wine is heavier now, more perfumed. She moves into the bedroom and undresses. She lies upon the bed and touches her sex. Her spasms are deep, made perfect by the power of imagination.

The lift arrives at the ground floor. I walk through the foyer into the light of rue Galande. Only a minute would have passed. She will still be in the main room, the muscadet poised at her lips.

In the street I turn towards her room, looking up. I know that someone standing, glass in hand, at the table would be visible, or become visible, to someone walking from this building and turning back. I stop. I search for her window, counting the floors upwards from the ground. It is empty.

✳ 3 ✳

Disconsolate return. A reckoning. Melbourne's early winter evening hatched through with rain; a view deleted, back and back. Another season, as perhaps it should have been, irreconcilable with beginnings.

The taxi winds its way along the freeway. Green and white signs: their destinations deadeningly familiar. My head is pressed against the rear side window. I watch the bulging lanterns of reflected carlights – these marquees strung against the glistening macadam of night – until my breath across the glass hazes everything from view.

The driver glances back to ask

our preference of route, the 'you'
enclosing us. This plurality I carry
with me everywhere. The burden of
her. I watch the pallor of her face
interrogated by oncoming traffic.
The downcast eyes. The lines that
grow from them like creases in
material: a pale crushed cotton that
has been half smoothed again. A
piteous attempt to repair an
accident.

The windscreen wipers screech
against the momentary break in fall.
Along the footpaths, dogs of trees
are shaking themselves free of rain.

On the hallway table there is a
bottle of champagne and a note
from Jeffrey. A welcoming home. I
carry the suitcases from the hallway
to the main bedroom. Everything is
familiar. As if I had left it the week
before and not these months. And
I had expected to return with eyes
that might enliven the quotidian.

Gillian has followed me into the

room. She has brought the carry-bags. I hear myself asking her if she would prefer me to sleep in the end room.

'Do what you want,' she can barely say.

'If that's what you want,' I reply.

Alone, again, the 'you' has split. Her declaration sets me free. I feel it moving to embrace me. Turning to the mirror. You are quite alone, it says.

MELBOURNE

Tuesday, June 12. The fifth day of persistent rain. Imbecilic falling. Gillian retires to her bedroom. Each evening this pointed withdrawal. When I pass by the door, always left ajar as if to offer the admission I have no desire to take, I see her, bolstered on the bed beneath her roses quilt: her face devoid of colour, vacuous, as if it were asleep apart from her. Her eyes have glazed like those of the shitting dogs.

From the study I can hear her move, occasionally, in the room. Or else I hear what seems to be a stifled cry. Perhaps she is pleasuring herself. Perhaps she simply cries aloud.

The lessons have begun again: a procession of arrivals after 4.00. The shrill child-voices, the endless repetition of the phrases: persistent as this rain.

I prefer to wait until she is asleep, but she is about some business still. Her precious voice ceased hours ago: a relentless *la-la-la-la-la-la-la* and then the shift a semitone. There is a certain blighting trace of tremolo – as if a keening might have crept into the delivery.

I have begun to smoke far more and in an increasingly expulsive manner. The study is permeated with blue air – a barrier to her entrance. Sometimes I arise from the desk to blow smoke down the hallway. On one occasion I blew smoke rings.

Alone in this room, every moment becomes drenched in the thought of sex. I turn the pages of these magazines. How quickly their surprise has dissipated. How little time before these images will fail to arouse, will lose this necessary excess.

In this particular photograph she is with two men. A written text accompanies the image, like the biographies of beggars chalked on the *correspondance* tunnels of the Metro.

    . . . *deux bites bien raides, c'est le minimum pour une nana comme moi. A peine pubère, ma chatte était déjà la partie la plus active de ma personne. C'est Georges qui m'a fait découvrir le plaisir d'être enculée. Je suis folle des deux activités. C'est pourquoi je ne laisse échapper aucun sand-wich quand l'occasion se présente . . .*

These stories we might choose to believe or disbelieve. These new biographies.

Her eyes meet mine. She fails to take her eyes from me. My gaze, as if encouraged by her own persist-ence, follows down her flesh, rest-ing at this fulcrum point of the double penetration: the three bodies locked together at this moment. I notice, for the first time, the presence of a wristwatch which has recorded, inadvertently, the actual instant of this encounter, locating it in history.

It is 10.26.

The men have filled her with their penises. They are absorbed in the act of penetration. But the woman, burdened with this cheap erotic name – Mimi – stares towards me. I become aroused. I crave her name in this other place. What shall I call her? Julia? Frances? Catherine?

And what has happened to her in the hours before 10.26? Did she rise at 7.00, still tired from the dancing of the previous night? Had she shaved? Had she showered, conscious of the photo session that morning involving anal penetration? And how has this affected her in matters of hygiene? What of her eating patterns for the preceding twenty-four hours? Were there foods she might have chosen to refuse for this reason alone? And what are these other necessary choices? Is she, for example, responsible for the choice of underwear and stockings? Does she select a pair of high-heeled shoes – their soles unscuffed – appropriate to wear in bed? This woman whose love expresses itself in complete abandon, here in this real world.

⁂ 2 ⁂

Paris
July 12

Avery, how brilliantly timed your letter! And I arriving home from England in the exhaustions and the sadnesses of a love affair now ended! You must imagine me entering my apartment with that dread, familiar and inescapable (and yet for which there is no preparation), of facing the near future alone. And there at my feet, slipped beneath my door by the concierge, your letter, waiting when I most needed you, confirming you a part of me, and with such audacious declarations!

And then, so sad, these words that speak of Paris as if she were a lover, lost forever. How can I comfort you? Should I ask you to recall the noise and rush, the streets stained with the litter of dogs or the urine of the *clochards*. No: whilst cursing her – as does everyone who lives here – I know there is no other place, and my cry joins with yours for this city with its beloved monotones of grey and grey-cream, its river and its flock of bridges. This plenitude: the columned arcades of Rivoli, the steam-filled windows of Rosier.

For a while I thought that it was London that enthralled me, but I realise now I had confused my feelings with the love of a man who lived there. I should have listened to the words of my friend Georges: the English are repressed, incapable of saying how they feel. 'I'm sorry,' says the lover, after eight months of involvement, even more, and still no closer, 'but I'm not too good at this.' Shrinking back. His words a 'mix of fear and guilt' (*his* words). I curse the race! I tell him, 'From now on you don't exist!'

How different this letter, with its openness (its forwardness!), its daring to be heard. Yet I also understand how, for those who know the great insanity that is passion, this city speaks through our voices and encourages us.

What is our crime, you wonder, that we should have met to part? Perhaps we shall discover this after time. As time might also reveal the judge and the enforcers of our punishment. What shall I say? Believe me, Avery, that I should take you as a criminal, hidden in these rooms. Of course: come and live *la bohème* in Paris. Just to write and love! (How many dream of this, who turn the pages of their Miller or their Scott Fitzgerald? Do you imagine *that* life still exists!) What is return if not gesture? If not surrender – absolute and unequivocal, a necessary shedding of the vestiges of past. And what holds you from this return? The cost of risk? The cost of guilt?

This afternoon the sun has reappeared, the cloud broken for the first time in six weeks. So there is promise of a summer; but as to its purpose?

Catherine

Paris
August 3

Once again this place has been born into humidity – only now have I remembered heat. Torpid days, the air almost drinkable. Endless transformations: windows opened and thrown wide.

The weather has made a carnival of the city. Yesterday I was with a friend at Le Rubis, an old-fashioned wine bar with pink and white neon curved high above its counter. Everyone was spilling from the mirrored walls into the street, around the corner into rue Saint-Hyacinthe. The warmth of the evening was like a man's hand on my breast. Suddenly we were invaded by Egyptians, their skins dyed

71

golden by the sun, their bodies
flaring with barbaric jewels! They
overflowed from taxis. They moved
amongst us, helping themselves
to our wine and to the wine of
others. They stole our *tartines*, then,
laughing, sped away. All is madness –
but this is only to be expected.

I realise I too have become barbaric here, my body left unclothed.
In the late dying light, in *l'orangerie*
of this apartment, I seem adrift. I
bathe my wrists in water and
cologne. I hear the distant scimitars
of voice, of traffic, as if the heat had
curved the noises of the street; the
wailing of sirens late into the night
a call to some devotion.

It occurs to me I have been
infected with that same restlessness
I detect in your letters – just as I am
exhausted by the rigours of search.
Yes, that afternoon has never left
me: the sense of possibilities
unfolding, closed by the inflexi-
bility of time and adamant circumstance.

The concierge has left for Nantes. With her departure, the old man from the second floor has once again emerged to deliver our mail. The two are like those wooden figurines that appear from clocks: the day, the night, each with their separate time.

This afternoon I came home to find him bent beneath the ochre light of the landing. I waited as his fingers sorted through the pile of envelopes. He held out your letter, hands trembling, his eyes averted, as if he were ashamed of what its pages might contain.

I have arranged to spend the third week of August in the south of France. I shall go to Collioure and seek the colours of the Fauvists. I shall eat braised mussels stuffed with sagemeat! I shall imagine it is we who are travelling through these places, returning late to a hotel, our lips swollen, our skin sticky with salt.

Montagnac
August 23

Imagine a running child, the disorder of hair across the forehead. It is how the ivy overhangs the small front gate of my house. I have been living in an isolated village (old stone dwellings perched on a hill overlooking a valley planted with vineyards) in the Languedoc, some forty kilometres from Montpellier. Behind the house there is a vast wild tangled garden from which one may observe the neighbour's child, Colombe, forever walking on the tar roof of their shed.

There are mostly old people in the village: life is very quiet here, except in summer when the English come. The days have been hot. Thirty-seven, thirty-eight degrees. In the evenings people sit outside till late: always the children running; the men in clusters, smoking, playing *pétanque*. I walk through the streets and drink with these accursed English. The young men ask me endless questions and each night I amuse myself inventing other pasts.

During the days I have been driving to a small beach between Agole and Sète. I undress slowly, exposing my body to the flame of the sun until the burning envelopes me and my whole being surges up to my skin.

One afternoon I made a pilgrimage to the Cimetière Marin in Sète to see Valéry's grave. I found I could still recite the opening verses of the poem from when I studied it in my final year at school. For a moment I was that young woman again, with her strength and happiness, poised before a life, only half sensed, in which I would be desired by men and have to survive that desire.

I remembered I had only ever seen a photograph of Valéry as a white-haired old man, and when he exhorted us to run to the waves and spring from them again alive, I had this vision of my uncle in his one-piece black bathing costume with straps over the shoulders in the thirties and his skinny white legs!

It is your letters that have enlivened me. For the first time in my life (you see, how even now there can be firsts) I have begun to know a man – and I talk here of that most intimate of knowledges – without first having slept with him. And I find it very exciting.

I say this because recently I have engaged in sex – and quite intemperately so – without emotion. Perhaps this is the cost I have exacted for my disappointment at a lack of commitment – the Englishman, for example. I have drawn my pleasures from them, certainly, but over the days these men merge into each other – they lose that singularity that makes us fall in love with them. You will not be like everyone else.

Which brings me to something you said in your last letter. Yes, it has changed. Something more wilful than these words has passed between us. These letters have the power to conjure, to tempt, and to arouse.

My husband used to say (with a certain touch of bitterness) I would make a better mistress than a wife, that I should have been born in another age and been a Ninon de Lenclos, or a professional *courtisane*. So be it.

In the house there are eleven windows showing between the ivy-covered wooden trellis. One shutter in the middle has been put there for symmetry only. I often think about this mysterious room which does not exist behind the closed shutter. Perhaps this is where we are meeting in these languid (and illicit) hours.

Paris
September 6

This afternoon: a wet, grey, suddenly autumnal time. I feel summer has now finally deserted us, its moment gone too soon.

I am in my bedroom, appropriately perhaps, reading your last letter and its bold requests. What a strange correspondence this has become, like some long slow enduring sex. How different the very touch of these pages: their first assertion in my hands; with time, their gradual softening.

It is as if, over these months, you have become more *present*. My sadness at your absence is that of a woman whose lover has returned that morning to his own apartment (and dare I say it: to his *wife*). It is the sadness of a parting that promises return.

As I write, I find myself awaiting your next letter (Such impatience! Is it possible to think it might be rewarded?), knowing that it must be at least two weeks for your reply. And there is nothing to be done about it! Still I prefer letters to the telephone. They remain, and you can reread them. They are part of the person who has written.

My mother and I corresponded every week for twenty years – and even though I moved all around the world, I always took her letters with me, crammed into airline bags and suitcases, and I still have them, although she is gone. Her last letters to me written in a child's hand, their sentences half finished . . .

Shall I tell you parts of my secret life? I recently met a young man who asked me to teach him everything I knew about sex. In addition to the more obvious requests, he gave me a list of some half-dozen perversities, saying, 'You can start with any one of these.' *Quel programme!* (One day I will tell you the list.)

I rather fancy myself in the role of *initiatrice*. It is, as you know, an old French tradition, and every young man needs an older woman who will teach him things without making any demands of him, and without expecting any more of the relationship than that. He will always remember her with affection because there will be no possessiveness or jealousy, just pure pleasure. I have already gone through two of the things on the list and he is delighted.

I of course believe that just as every young man needs an older woman, so does every married man need a mistress, and every married woman a lover. Otherwise desire dies: that desire at least which is like a fire that burns you, and keeps you on the edge in what is almost a state of agony, because the longing is so intense.

One of the reasons I walked out on my marriage (which in many ways was a good one) was that the desire had gone. I said, I want to wait for my lover like a child waits for Christmas Day – with that same excitement and anticipation. And when he is five minutes late it is unbearable.

Imagine us together here. Think of all the things we would talk about, all the things that you might want to know, all the things that you might dare to ask of me.

Paris
September 23

What has led me to such impetuous correspondence? All through my life I have sought experience, sensation, pleasure, intensity – and for these reasons, particularly the latter, there must be constant renewal. My search has led me very far. When old age approaches, I must, at least, have no regrets, no feeling of 'if only I had done . . . ' That would be intolerable.

Since I freed myself of marriage, and with my daughter grown up and gone, I can live as I please, without the need to answer to anyone, or to justify or excuse my actions. I have been through periods of euphoria and despair, of extraordinary highs and limitless fantasy, of self-indulgence. And always the desire to go further, to push back the limits, to be unafraid. You can imagine that sometimes I feel there is nothing new, and yet there is, and hence the challenge and the fascination – this *liaison épistolaire!* I have never done it before and it excites me, yes, in a real way, and tantalises, because it leaves the imagination free.

One of the things on the list was his desire to tie me up. Not in a banal way – this was with that wide, shiny sticky-tape that is used to close boxes and parcels. I was bound tightly from the feet up to my neck (as in the bandages of an Egyptian mummy), my arms pinned to my sides, with only my breasts and sex uncovered. I couldn't move or stand or sit, and I could hardly breathe.

First of all, he spent the necessary time exciting me with his mouth.

Then he climbed astride me, mounting my face. Like so many men I have known, he has a particular enthusiasm for spilling his seed in any place apart from where is commonly seen as 'natural'. Afterwards I watched him slowly turn my silent face. I could see him gaze at me; wishing to understand everything, to draw every pleasure from me.

I will tell you the next thing on the list in another letter – that is, if you want to hear. I am beginning to believe what some men have told me – that is, that I am too *extreme*. I remember your first letter: 'I have always sought a woman whose love expresses itself in total abandon.' I am tired of these liars and these cowards. Let us exalt in our excess!

I shall close now, in order that this reach you more quickly. I want your reply. I want to hear if these things have pleased you.

Paris
October 10

So many questions I hardly know where to begin. Perhaps with a maxim: '*la tendresse est le contraire de l'érotisme*'.

These perversities in which we take such evident delight would be unthinkable within a marriage. And not because the other might not enjoy them, but because they are ultimately excluded by familiarity. It happened to me – that is why I took so many lovers in my years of marriage.

The first few months, or even less, establishes the acts in which the couple will engage. And who would sensibly admit something perverse, especially when this might well jeopardise the relationship that is so desired! (You see how privileged we are – to have this opportunity to speak our uttermost desires.) And then, of course, it has become too late. To speak of something *now* would saturate it with significance. Imagine if the wife should suddenly express a wish for anal intercourse. She thinks about this every day, imagining the fullness of this penetration. But how would such an aberration be explained within the marriage? 'What has changed?' the other asks. 'Why this desire, so suddenly, so unpredictably, manifested?' No, for most relationships there is the prospect of a slow decline towards the ordinary.

Against this, pure eroticism is detached, cerebral – it is lived in what I call the *huis-clos de l'amour*. It is what I have with my young man. With him I play games, but I never really make love.

Another of the things on his list was a *ménage* with a third person. This was easy to arrange because I have an old friend and lover who had already initiated me into this particular perversity. I call him my Valmont, and I am his Marquise. I sometimes think we are rather wicked the way we have lured unsuspecting men (so far it has been men – I don't know how I might function with a woman) into our trap. There are so many possibilities: either they both make love to me at the same time, and that I find is ecstasy – those extra hands and mouths and penises all at once – or, if one of them is tired, or waiting to recover, he will sit back and watch me with the other.

So, I arranged for my friend to come over one time when my young man was here, and he was delighted – uninhibited, natural, spontaneous. You would never have thought that it was the first time for him!

For sex to be really good, I must let my feelings become involved. I must be in love, even though most men are afraid of women falling in love with them because they see it as a loss of freedom. But I don't know where sex ends and love begins – they merge and become the same thing. If a man makes good love to me, I fall in love with him. It is also true though, that if the sex is not good I will *never* fall in love.

And what is love to a man?

Paris
October 29

The evening is approaching. I am travelling in a country train on its return to Paris. Perhaps it is moving through Normandy – yes, we are passing by a village with its black and white half-timbered houses.

A stranger now appears at the glass of my compartment. He lifts his briefcase into the luggage rack and takes a seat directly opposite me. We talk for only minutes before his mouth and hands have sought me. Now he enters me. I am fully clothed – he has simply torn aside the loose material. At any moment someone may pass by on their way to the WC – so much the better, that they should see such fierce coupling!

It is over quickly. There has been perhaps a slight brutality about it. Afterwards the man returns to his seat and takes the paper from his case. As for myself, I return to this familiar view. It is a fantasy I have entertained for many years and only once have realised.

How often I have seen myself a sister to Anaïs: living only for ecstasy, extravagance; all moderate love, half-shades, leaving me cold! But only now have I begun to realise the extent of this desire. I tremble at the abyss of my passions.

As for this letter you describe – so explicit, so extreme, that at the moment of its first description the reader might ejaculate across its pages – is it not the condition to which all writing has aspired? Demanding that admission of desire (no matter how unlikely, how unspeakable), an honesty, so absolute it would produce a masterpiece.

Shall I continue with my list? By way of preparation my young lover had me shave my genitals: an act which he observed with considerable fascination. Of course, I have often indulged myself this way. Only shaved does one feel completely naked and exposed. Even when dressed, the materials caress you constantly – at times almost unbearably so. Furthermore, I love to see the shock it gives to men, when you undress in front of them, to see the folds of your sex so prominently displayed.

In such a state he entered me – but with his hand, which I accepted to the wrist; and near my final climax, he has told me, to the forearm.

You wonder if perhaps I have made you the voyeur, but for me it is rather that you are *present* at these moments, not an observer of them. For me, his unforgiving

penetrations are the moments when
I feel you moving deep within me:
both present and not present.

Avery, I know that your release
will surely come. And it shall be my
face that is there before you,
waiting.

Paris
November 16

This afternoon I lunched with
Clare. She enquired as to whether
we had kept in touch. I know of her
suspicions; she has known me too
long. But what could have possibly
transpired between us now, after
five months and at such a distance?
Perhaps it is because the mention of
you has quickened me. Perhaps my
hand has moved involuntarily to
touch myself.

How frightening this need to tell!
How important and how dangerous
this talisman that is the beloved's
name! The exquisiteness of hearing

it, of speaking it aloud. This holy blasphemy. This obscenity. This world! And how difficult it must be for you – bound by this passion – without the ability, the opportunity, to speak it or express it!

But you are right. Only the *speaking* of these desires can destroy us: it is the weak point from which our acts unravel. And yet how it begs to be released. That is why our writing has undergone these changes. Why I have pressed your letters hard against my sex and brought them back to my eyes almost unreadable!

Your questions are so persistent – again I ask myself if it is true that we can exhaust these possibilities. Do we become jaded? Do we want more and more extreme things? Do we reach the point where 'normal' sex is not enough? Is too insipid? I know women of my age, whose lives had been characterised by promiscuity, who now have abandoned sex entirely. For

some, even the *company* of men has
become intolerable. They seek
some other future: a return to some
lost dignity.

Perhaps I have this fear of bore-
dom, so I find myself playing com-
plicated games in order to keep
desire alive. I don't want to see a
man every day, I want to avoid
routine. I must build up the desire
for him by letting a day or two go
by, and really start wanting him
again. It is how I await your letters – as I might a lover, never
knowing exactly when he will
arrive, never sure of what demands
I must fulfil.

Your last letter begs me to continue with the list. Can you imagine
what it might possibly be? Perhaps
it is what you have wanted me to
describe for some months but have
been frightened to ask. Remember,
I am your mistress. You may ask
anything of me.

My young lover had expressed a
wish to watch me urinate. This

came as no surprise to me, as it would not, I should imagine, to you either. The act is quite essential to the erotic: the turning of our private acts into a public spectacle.

For my display I chose to lie naked in my bath, my legs across the edges of the enamel. So prepared, I called his name. Imagine how it would have appeared to him entering from the main room to see me thus: fingers holding apart the fullness of my flesh and the fluid breaking from me! Is this sufficient? Do you wish more detail? Shall I tell you how I slid my shoulders back down the bath, my hair resting in the pungent warmth, and raised my legs high above my body in the position of the exercise called bicycling. Shall I describe how the next spasm shot from me high in the air, covering my whole body in its fall, blinding me. And how I stayed like this until I had quite utterly soaked myself in front of him. Shall I describe how it was in this blinded state that I felt his fruit shed its seed, melting in *jouissance*, changing its absence into delight in my mouth, where its shape died!

Or do you wish, as I suspect, for even more? Far more?

Paris
December 3

How your description fills me with unbearable longing. The extremity of your passion. I too can no longer sleep. My mouth craves the taste of you. As I eat, as I drink, I imagine these foods have been pushed from your body. I hold them in my mouth, I swallow them, occasionally I squeeze them through my teeth and lips and watch them fall back to the tablecloth. I am a savage here, alone in this room. Only yesterday for example, having felt the urge to urinate, I simply wet myself. I lit a cigarette and leant back in the chair watching the material darkening between my legs.

Avery, we are only doing what all lovers might wish to do (perhaps their acts do not have the courage of ours, nor do they have the wealth of our imaginings), except we have not chosen to keep our wishes secret from each other.

Even Jean-Philippe. (So, I have inadvertently written his name. I cannot be bothered to erase it – the name I cry is yours alone.) I shall describe in detail what happened recently. The act was not in fact on his original list. I suspect he wished it from the very start, but could not bring himself to admit it – how timid we are, how reluctant to expose that which we most desire. How many must go their entire lives unfulfilled. But now it seems as if these other activities had just been preparations for this newest act. As if, having been taught the necessary skills, he was ready to spread his wings; to reveal his own, deeper desires.

His initial request was that I lie, eyes closed, upon my bed, my legs tied wide apart, secured to the bed posts. After binding me, I heard him leave the room. There was the sound of the locks on his case, then he returned. I felt the slow movement of his fingers working lubricant into my sex. Then I felt an object introduced deep inside me, cold and rounded at its end, then more awkwardly shaped, narrowing then broadening to a width that pulled hard against my flesh. I felt him move this object back and forth in minute movements, as if his hand were shaking with some terrible palsy. I heard him cry aloud and opened my eyes. He was crouched beside me, his fingers slathered with ejaculant. Unsure, I watched him draw the object slowly from me, until I saw the bald, streaming head of a doll.

Avery, I have come more and more to understand this: nothing can watch over us if what we wish is full of sin. We must search for these beautiful obscenities alone and we alone must face the consequences and the judgment that will surely follow.

I await you in this other place, other city. Come to me, to everything that has been written. Kiss the dark sex of me.

Can we not sustain ourselves forever like this, surrendering to these pages, our lives endlessly rewritten. Imagine everything you wish to happen at this moment of our meeting, *poète*, and it shall happen.

❋ 3 ❋

I come to her. She is lying on her belly, hands behind her back, palms flattened on her buttocks. She pulls the spheres of flesh apart, exposing

the darkened iris. I lick its creases.
Myriad. Bitter. Her genitals are
shaved: it is as if I were seeing the
sex of a woman for the first time.
My finger runs within the folds of
flesh. Anticipation has already
soaked her. Still, I take the lubricant
and smother my hand to the wrist.
She turns. I catch the movement,
and in response add more jelly,
massaging hand, wrist, and now the
forearm into a familiar of the penis.
My fingers form their beak: I am the
swan head, entering her; I am the
neck. Occasionally she reaches back
to caution, to withhold the thrusting to the forearm. I take her hand
and place the fingers at the clitoris,
requiring her to pleasure herself in
front of me. She begins to rub, as
if she were seeking to erase her sex.
She comes, wind breaking from her
at my wrist. Now her face is upside
down before me. I trace the circle
of this loose inverted mouth. I
smear the lipstick back as if to
enlarge its opening. My penis rests

across her face. I watch how it is silvering her neck. I kneel astride her head, lowering the scrotum into her mouth. I watch the hollowing and rehollowing of her cheeks. I withdraw, watching her fingers search out the hairs, her tongue sucking at the roof of her mouth. One by one she produces them: seven in all. The smear of lips now closes round my penis, the motion of her mouth awakening in me a similar motion, as if transmitted by contagion. She reaches back and enters me. I feel her pushing deep inside: two fingers, crossed slightly, almost to the webbing. She trills. I feel a spasming. My penis levers from her mouth. Her hand has followed it, the palm curving, pressing at the eye. A jet of urine shoots involuntarily from me, brindling her ribs and belly. I reach down and swirl the liquid, bringing it to her breasts. Her cries alone have nearly brought me to ejaculation. Now we stand facing each other. Rills of liquid trickle down her body. We are immaculate, in awe and wonder of each other's body. I tremble, heavy with the weight of the sperm inside me. Now she is kneeling in between my legs, drawing my knees upwards. She loops her arms beneath them, swinging my legs back above my shoulders; my penis only inches from my face. She takes my hand, placing it upon the shaft, moving it back and forward, inviting me to masturbate as I had *her*. I watch the skin drawn back across the head. Her fingers have re-entered me. Her mouth sucks at the base of my testicles. I spasm uncontrollably, pasting her fingertips with excrement. She withdraws. I watch her slowly daub the strokes of my initial on her breast. I am unsure what blinds me first to this vision. But now the sperm, in its second and its third expulsions, gathers in my mouth. I exalt in the unexpected warmth of my own release. She lowers me back to the mattress. We kiss deeply – as we had that afternoon in May – my hands entwined amongst the auburn of her hair.

I open my eyes, instead, to Gillian's face. It partakes of a strange devotion: radiant, serene, as if in contemplation of some holy object. As if the semen I had just expelled inside her passive belly had cured her of this illness.

How still we have both become, perhaps having momentarily fallen into sleep. I gaze at the white fleshes of our bodies together on this bed. A porcelain of limbs. There is silence. The absolute silence of the photograph.

And then from somewhere well beyond the border of this place, the first trace of sound begins, the faintest hum of traffic moving through the streets. Through the narrowness of these *ruelles*, the grandeur of these boulevards.

SOREL ATHERTON

APORIA

Aporia is a figure whereby the speaker sheweth that he doubteth, either where to begin for the multitude of matters, or what to do or say in some strange ambiguous thing.

A Book of Rhetoric, *1657*

❊ 1 ❊

Where to begin? If the reply had never come from France, I might have started with my memory of Chris's face – pale fruit, half eaten – that is, if not for the novella, if not for everything that Jeremy had finally said. You see, I wrote to 'Catherine'.

I always *had* the address. Chris knew this, had chosen to describe her writing it on the back of a bookmark and passing it to me in our shared taxicab. The Abbey Bookshop: refuge for the poet, scholar, pilgrim. It *says* that. I still have it, here, in my hand. How did he put it – 'this address I have repeated to myself a thousand times!' Then there are the things I shall never know, and those that are imponderable: why he had to tell this story at all, what he might eventually have done with it. Finally, the deeper questions. How long would he have maintained the lie of change, the lie of sex? These are things to which I shall return.

Of course, I forget how once there wasn't any *telling* of our lives (and let me disregard the way this telling has presented me: 'It is all false, false, false!'), but just our lives. Into a part of which, into the part I'd taken for a new beginning (the change I mentioned only sentences ago), came that most terrible of interruptions: the simple ringing of a telephone.

By then it was already written – like some other darkness, fully formed, concealed, awaiting its disclosure. Just as you have seen it. As to the means by which this came to light, it began, significantly enough, with a letter.

Hawthorn
January 20

Dear Sorel,

Just a brief note: first, to let you know you are in my thoughts, and, should you feel the need to talk, or simply have some company, that you are welcome here at any time.

The other thing – I realise it's not what you might want to be bothered

with at this time – is I would like
to publish Christopher's novella in
the autumn *Métier*. (I had thought
originally of spreading it across two
or three issues, but I felt it would
be good to bring this out whilst he
is here with us.)

Of course, I will be absolutely
guided by your wishes in this matter
and would not want to proceed
without your blessing.

Please let me know. Maybe you
would like to have dinner one night?
We seem to see so little of each
other these days.

Jeremy Fayrfax

I find this appalling to write – I
burn, my face burns, even though I
am alone, even though I am totally
unobserved. My body burns – *I
knew nothing of a novella*.

There was a change. At the beginning of December, he began to speak of a rebuilding. One that could not, should not, be rushed, because of the damage that had already been done, that *he* had done.

Those months after our return from France, night after night I'd glimpse him moving by the doorway, the floorboards betraying every movement, to his study. I'd lie there, waiting for this possible return. I would exhaust myself, month upon month.

Then quite inexplicably: his presence. He came to me, at first, to ask forgiveness, and, after seven days or so . . . How can I possibly talk about it, knowing now what had enlivened him? He came to me. I was lying in bed on that most ordinary warm December evening, and he kissed me, the touch of his fingers making me cry out, quite inadvertently.

The telephone began to ring just

before 11.00 in the morning. (He had waited for the traffic to clear before leaving for the university.) At the time I was pulling down the bed. The words were functional and in a woman's voice – a nurse's – and spoken with the calm that accompanies the dreadful, the unspeakable.

Absurdly, it appears in retrospect, I found myself listening for him in the background. But there was too much talking, too much laughter – the sounds, it seemed, of Hell.

I must have asked what had happened, because the voice was saying that he was unconscious and was having tests: the doctor would be able to give me further information. It was saying I should come to the hospital, to the casualty department. It was giving me the address.

I read it. Just as you have read it. The first time. How it is, there.

Under other circumstances (if Christopher had lived), how would this book be different? If, and if, and if . . . In the padded envelope with Jeremy's brief covering note. As I saw, not then of course; as I thought I saw later; and as, later, I began to see.

I recognised everything. Not *everything*; I mean, I recognised everything in which I had a direct part. My first reading was full of the pain of memory: I had forgotten the minutiae of our time in France, if not the silences. (It was the force of hatred underpinning them I hadn't known.)

I recognised Catherine. Not, of course, that this is her name, any more than my name is Gillian, or Christopher's is Avery.

I was shown to a waiting-room and took a seat amongst a group of people – I hardly noticed their number, only that there seemed so many. I remember feeling that the largeness of this group might adversely affect his chances of recovery. Most were women, alone, or with children. Those who were in company sat huddled, engaged in anxious conversation: endless speculations; guesses based on fear or hope, on misunderstandings of what the body can and cannot survive.

I knelt before the wardrobe. I pulled out the bottom right-hand drawer and removed my journal, watching the ribboned letters that the book had previously supported topple to the side. The trace of lavender came to me again. This persistence. I turned to Thursday, May 10, the day of Sainte Solange, to find that we had stayed in Châtel-Guyon at the Hôtel Bellevue, and the following day, the day of Sainte Estelle, in Autun, at the Hôtel Moderne. I found that on May 24, Ascension, we had a dinner invitation from Kate Metherall and her husband, Jean-Luc, to meet the novelist Harry Mathews, and his partner, Marie Chaix. And Frances Bourin.

I began to wonder, if all *this* was so precise, why he should turn with such fierceness, and with such obsessive detail, to invention.

I watched the doctor (I'd thought others, previously, to be the doctor, but this was not to prove the case) verifying with the duty nurse, then walk up to where I was seated. What should he call me? Was I Mrs Houghton or Miss Atherton? I told him I'd chosen to retain my maiden name.

He invited me away from the others.

'We think your husband's had a stroke. We've done a CT – a scan – which shows a large haemorrhage into the left side of the brain.'

I asked if he was going to die.

I read the version of my acquiescence to his afternoon with Catherine: how it seemed I was willing it to take place. But I remember thinking at the time that if this should happen – even something as clear as an afternoon of lovemaking – then I did not want to be blamed for having prevented it.

On his return, he seemed quite flushed, not only, I felt, from the wine (I could smell the wine) and the walk from her apartment on such a warm day. There was a breathless exhilaration to him. The exhilaration of sin, perhaps. I didn't mention 'the afternoon', but he chose, almost immediately, to be dismissive of it. It was 'fine', or something similar – even this seemed extravagant conversation. Or else he was readying himself for Geoffrey's imminent arrival – you see, we had arranged to pick him up at Charles de Gaulle by 4.30. But the manuscript has already told you that.

Christopher, I wondered time and time again, where were the drafts, the different versions of the letters, the record of research? What would show me where you learned the weather patterns in Paris for the weeks immediately after our departure, the constant cloud and then the sudden change?

Because I knew of your research of the Cathédrale Saint-Lazare. I recognised the devil and his baubled hair like so many Christmas bells. I recognised the cold, the chlorine cold of the stone. I had stared too long at this apparition, until the sound of your approaching feet disturbed me.

Then I did this, actually had to do this: I took the morning's paper and sought out the weather page. There, below the heading 'World',

I read for Paris: 'Rain, 10–12'.

But what of a village in the Languedoc, forty kilometres from Montpellier?

A pettiness, of course. The narrative demands the day be hot – then let us call it thirty-seven, thirty-eight degrees! What's more, in such a provincial town they play *pétanque* – one hardly needs the Larousse for this. Nor for the Fauvist colours at Collioure. Nor the young Englishmen with all their questions on her life – and all her lies. Nor to have this woman with the name of Catherine, having returned from a nightly walk, retire to her bedroom to compose a letter.

Of course it is all fiction. Not only does one betray his art, but all art by reducing it to mere transcription.

But then, what about the town of Agole?

In a series of small steps, not unlike

a dance, the doctor had shifted his body between the rows of chairs and my line of vision, shielding me, possibly, from the gaze of the waiting women. I suppose it was an awkward question I'd asked anyway.

'He's unconscious at the moment,' he replied, edging slightly backwards on the hard linoleum squares. 'We know it's serious. He's been examined by the neurosurgeons. They don't think an operation would help.'

I remember waiting at every moment for the sentence to be given, only to find a series of postponements. Then he had stopped, with a half-embarrassed smile, a pulling wide of the lips (looking back, it may well have been an involuntary nervous act), hoping perhaps this might suffice as an answer. Possibly I wasn't expected to respond.

'So what is going to happen?'

'We have to wait. Watch, over

the next couple of days. In this type
of situation many don't wake up.
You can't really predict for any
particular person . . . '

He paused. Perhaps he'd taken
pity on me.

'There is a chance he could die.
On average, roughly a third of
patients in his condition will die, a
third will be damaged, a third
recover.'

I wanted suddenly to know what
'damaged' meant. I was terrified by
the very sound of it. It struck me
as a hideous word; an ugly, sicken-
ing thing.

He said he loved me.

There was a change in him, quite
unaccountable, for which I only
had his words – his word – and I
believed him. It was this last des-
pairing act of faith.

I had wanted his love so long, and

for so long I'd watched him perfect a self-loathing, a self-absorption: a type of deprecation that craves denial from the other, which exhausted me. He preened, constantly believing in his capacity to captivate women whilst fervently denying his ability to do so, only to be reduced to despair when what he said would happen actually occurred.

But in my stupidity, I continued above all else to care for this man, and to expect from him what he'd failed to offer year after year.

'For example, he might experience difficulty in speaking or understanding,' the doctor offered. 'Maybe he'll be able to hear us and not be able to respond . . . '

I asked if it were possible to see him.

'Of course,' the doctor said. 'I did mention, didn't I, that he's still unconscious. The other thing you'll need to be aware of is that he'll be attached to a number of tubes – to help with breathing – and some drips, so you shouldn't be at all alarmed by his appearance. Okay?' He nodded, in apparent agreement with his own warning.

I found myself being led, half by the arm as one might lead an invalid, past the waiting area to a cubicle. We entered through a partition in the curtain.

Christopher was propped up on a trolley of sorts, with metal sides, like a cot. His mouth was covered by an oxygen mask which had drifted slightly askew. The doctor stepped towards the bed and moved the mask. I watched it slowly slip back to its previous position.

There was a drip feeding into his left arm, which lay outside the covers like a toy of some description – a favourite animal, perhaps – and a flat bag beside the bed, fed by tubing which came from underneath the covers, filled with, I assume, his urine.

'I'll just leave you for a while,' the doctor was saying. 'You can talk if you like.' I found myself thanking him, quite out of habit, for this favour.

Where does the end begin? Was there ever a point where it might have been reversible? Or does that moment always elude us? Even when we search backwards for. it, armed with our histories, our documents, our photographs. Our re-evaluated memories.

I can remember thinking, because of this proliferation, because it seems that everything is brought to every other thing, this time shall have no end, because it cannot end . . .

I couldn't explain the change, but there was change. He was asking for forgiveness. No, nothing had happened, he was reassuring. He was asking me to forgive him for what he'd been for so long, especially the time in France, and before, as if he'd made some dreadful mistake. And how was it possible he hadn't always loved me? There was an articulateness about this analysis of his emotions, so uncharacteristic (indeed, the answers he gave to my questions lacked, almost totally, this eloquence) that I might have thought it quite prepared.

So it was, eventually, he entered our bed again, for the first time in almost seven months, and he wept.

Of course the doctor hadn't heard. He returned because a certain time had passed, or he was free from what had occupied him for those minutes.

'Everything okay?' he asked.

I nodded.

'Good.' He paused. 'We'll be shifting your husband to West

Ward shortly. You might like to get a coffee while we settle him in. Just before you do, there are some details you might be able to give us: whether he's on any medication at the moment. Blood pressure, heart problems? Any allergies? That sort of thing.'

On the weekend I began to search the house, looking everywhere for evidence – anything to convince me that the manuscript was fiction, not biography – leaving the study, which I saw to be my greatest hope, till last.

There were, of course, familiar things. The chairs each wearing clothing – the jacket with the leather patches, the grey-blue sleeveless jumper with the pockets for cigarettes and lighter. The books he'd brought back from Paris – Mathews, Salter (those so well known in this real world they'd been granted the privilege of

retaining their own names), La
Clos; a Balzac, *The Unknown Masterpiece*. Otherwise the room was
still a private diary, full of things
kept separate from our relationship:
the photos of a past preceding me;
letters scribbled in unknown, often
childlike, hands; a pipe; a legless toy
knight made of lead . . .

Then over the days these new lives,
these wilful biographies, drew a
kind of strength from doubt; began
to animate, grow fierce; began
increasingly to threaten me. Doubt
was the nature of my betrayal, and
I shall never forgive myself for that,
irrespective of what eventually I
came to learn.

So it was that the 'real' brought
its pack against the work of art,
began to run it down, to savage it.

'During the days I have been driving
to a small beach between Agole and

Sète. I undress slowly, exposing my body to the flame of the sun . . . '

Because – and I was *thorough* – everything that could be verified was verified, but nothing could be found that might *not* have happened. Except when I sought the road maps from the cardboard box inside the wardrobe – the box with all the postcards and the entry tickets – when I turned to page 106, which showed the beaches between Agole and Sète, there was no Agole.

Instead there was a town named Agde. This strange weak point in the telling of the story worried me. I stared at a brief stretch of coastline, I reread its single mention in that August letter. I tried to imagine why Christopher might have chosen to include in a work of scrupulous research a single town that didn't exist.

It seemed quite inconceivable that one might mistype the letters 'o' and 'l' for a single 'd'. Then, there was a frightening moment at a very simple thought (after all, to the English-speaking mind, is not the town Agole more likely than the quite improbable and unpronounce-able Agde?) that the invention of Agole might most easily be explained by the transcription of a misread hand.

I know the difference between art and life. I've been used to seeing art betray life, time and time again, to appropriate the necessary details. But this was different. This seemed as though life had now begun its own betrayal.

Betrayals. So many of them. Not only this. It is what we all have done. What I have done. What Frances did. What Christopher was doing, what he did. What Jeremy has done, and did. These tenses, these acts. Their repercussions.

I didn't return to the box immediately. I remember postponing the
moment for some hours: there were
several things that needed to be
done in any case. It was necessary
that I practise the *Chanson Italienne*
of Ravel, a piece that presents
certain difficulties for the soprano:
the refining of emotion to achieve
simplicity, the sustaining of the
vocal line. How does one sing for
so long if one is crying?

I always had the address. Written on
a bookmark and passed to me in the
back of a taxicab outside Geoffrey's
apartment.

It was in the cardboard box with
the other paraphernalia. 'The Abbey
Bookshop – Paris' best selection of
new and used scholarly and literary
English language books.' The red-
brown card with the geometric
motif in the corners.

I turned it slowly. In her hand
I read: Frances Bourin; 23, rue

Galanole, 5e. Except there is no rue Galanole in the fifth *arrondissement* or, for that matter, in Paris. Only rue Galande.

❋ 2 ❋

As friends they would have spoken of it – meeting almost every day at the department, speaking of it time and time again. After all, it was their job to speak of literature.

I sought out Jeremy's letter and chose the phrase to which I might respond – 'to have dinner one night' – and I rang. He suggested that it might be 'easier' if we were to eat at his house. 'Rather than, you know, with all those other people. I think we both might need a bit of quiet. Let's say Tuesday: 7.30 for 8.00?'

The slight curve at the edges, at the turnings of the corridors, gave the feeling momentarily that I was on board an ocean liner and returning to the cabin.

My footsteps hit at the linoleum. It seemed the only sound above a dully distant hum. I walked some thirty metres towards the dark space at the end of the corridor, and came to rest. I remember the increasing feeling that I was watching myself. Or was it more that I was watching someone else going through these moments? I pressed down the metal handle.

Christopher was lying in the bed, propped slightly to one side, the cot-sides up. A plastic bag, full of some faint brown liquid, hung from the wall to the right of him – a tube running from it, taped across his face, feeding to his nostril. His right arm was flexed and resting outside the covers of the sheet. He had been dressed in flannelette pyjamas: white with a faded two-green check. His hair had been combed, but differently than usual. They had given him a parting.

The lounge was much as I remembered it from those obligatory visits I'd made with Christopher over the years. The renovations had of course progressed. Both ceiling and walls had been ragged: a mottling of parchment and a blue (almost ice) down to the picture rail; and below, the parchment mixed with slates and greys and charcoals. Within the room, only the settee – draped in its blue-grey covers – seemed 'unfinished'.

The day had been oppressive: a fierce, still Melbourne day, one of the first of summer. The house retained an airless warmth. Possibly the windows were open, but, even with the light, the curtains had been drawn.

'It's not normally this tidy,' he seemed to be apologising. 'Mrs

Sinclair's been today.'

There was a constant flurry to his movements, of which he must have been aware but failed to keep under control. He would sit back in a lounge chair, legs crossed, and take a mouthful of champagne (he was offering champagne as though in celebration of something he had yet to reveal: a *brut taché*, the liquid stained a slightly crimson pink), and ask a question, which he would suddenly interrupt with an amusing anecdote or some unnecessary *double entendre*. There were gestures, actings out, and small dramatisations. He'd be off the chair, or perching on its edge, then out to the kitchen, or at the bookshelf. Or he'd be reminded of a track from a CD, or from a record, I must hear. He had the frantic lunacy of a moth – you half expected dust to smoulder from him, brushing past your chair – hell-bent on some collision.

There was too much food.

Appetisers from a gourmet delica-
tessen spread out across the low
cane table. Behind them loomed a
vase filled with exotic flowers I'd
never seen before, prompting me to
ask their name.

'Tulips,' he replied, smiling.
'One simply forces them open!
Anyway, Sorel, despite the awful
circumstances, it's lovely seeing you
again.'

I took the drink. I brought it to
my lips because some conciliatory
gesture seemed necessary. Above all
else, I couldn't start the evening
with refusal.

'Jeremy, I'm here about the
manuscript.'

'I'd imagined so,' he said. 'When
I sent it . . . I mean, it seems
incredible that Christopher had
never shown it to you.'

I waited.

'It's about us, of course.'

'I see.'

'Not entirely about us.' I heard
my words – neither question nor
statement – in fear, already, of

their repercussions.

'Of course not.'

'Look, it's all right. It just seems you're aware of more of this than I am. Perhaps you should assume complete ignorance on my part and tell me everything you know.'

My request seemed to have surprised him, silenced him.

'About what? I mean, what aspect?'

'Did you know he was writing this?'

'Well, not necessarily *this*. I knew he was working on something – I assumed everyone did. He seemed to be forever at the keyboard in his office.'

'Do you remember when he first mentioned it?'

'I suppose a month, or maybe two, after you got back from France.'

'And did he say what it was about? A hint?'

'No, not specifically. He said he was working on an idea for a prose piece . . . Look, do you want to sit up? I'll need to serve the vegetables presently.'

'I'm not really very hungry, I'm afraid, Jeremy.'

'Just have a taste. And I've got a wonderful red to have with it – it's a bugger about the weather, I was counting on that change – I've been saving this for years.'

It was strange. It seemed as though he'd totally misjudged the situation – his gestures tuned for another sort of evening – and was incapable of making the necessary adjustment.

I might have started with my memory of Chris's face. Its looseness, how it was somehow incomplete, the almost halfness of it. The ashen colour of the flesh. His slightly teary, waxy eyes, moving with their purposeless gaze away from me, or over me: it hardly mattered.

I found that I was staring at him from where I'd been seated. The pale brown curls of hair finely stroked with grey. The ginger beard also greying, but in tufts, not unlike a mould. The right eye with its slightest cast.

'Chris offered me the manuscript around the middle of December, only days before the stroke thing, the haemorrhage. You know, I was thinking about this the other day; it was about a week after that dreadful headache when he went home from work. I suppose that must have been related. And I remember he handed it to me with some line like "It's done." But as for drafts, I never saw any. I assume he transcribed everything he had, then did the necessary editing on disk.'

I could smell his breath from where I sat, carrying its own stale heat, its own quite palpable humidity.

'Did he keep a journal, do you know, Jeremy? On Paris, for

instance? I lived with him those months and I'd watch him writing, but I assumed that he was working on the poems. I'm not sure if he might have kept it from me, or I failed to see it, or whether in fact such a thing was never written.'

'I've no idea,' he said, and shrugged quite helplessly. 'He never mentioned it to me.'

'It's just that when you said that he'd transcribed everything, I wondered what it was he may have been transcribing?'

The cream light, coupled with the stillness, gave a painterly quality to the room those later hours. The noises from outside, lessening with the arrival of night, were finally lost beneath this ragged breathing and the constant hissing of the mask. I closed my eyes. I doubt that I was expecting sleep. From the carpet – held beneath this industrial perfume, the persistent trace of disinfectant – I could detect a palimpsest of odour, the stenches of excreta and of uncontrollable release. It was the smell of weakness.

I eased my position. I leant slightly to the left and peered through the lifted blind, cupping out the lamplight from the room. I could not imagine a sky containing more darkness. I sat like this a moment until I realised the rough edges of the breathing had become a rasp.

Whatever evening he'd planned, whatever he'd hoped to have transpire over those few hours, was in tatters.

The table was littered with half-finished objects: the bottle of champagne, the French stick and the Bordeaux, the inappropriate *boeuf bourgignon*, my glass of red – though this was quite untouched.

We'd been taken far away from all of this: the meal, some bizarre *Marie Celeste* artefact.

'He told me this much one evening – early, mid-November – that he'd met a woman in Paris and that they'd been writing to each other. That their letters had become increasingly erotic.'

His face had paled with sweat.

'Of course, Chris was a writer. It's possible that he'd invented the exchange in its entirety to test, you know . . . to see if it was believable.'

'And did *you* find it believable?'

As I leant forward from the settee, Jeremy slumped, in some foretaste of his dotage, back into the armchair.

'Yes,' he said. 'I believed him.'

I watched his hand swaying close beside the glass of Bordeaux.

'Did he say her name?'

'No. Nothing else. I found the whole thing dreadfully awkward. It wasn't a conversation I particularly wanted to encourage.'

'And when he gave you the manuscript?'

'When he gave me the manuscript, I took it, rightly or wrongly, for a *roman-à-clef*. I'm sorry.'

'Jeremy,' I said, finding I had said it sternly, as though to a transgressing child, 'was there anything else?'

He stood up. He might have been broad-shouldered were he not blighted by a stoop. Possibly he considered he was rising to an occasion, but the effect was more of cowered exhaustion. There was, I recall, an immense silence – one I feared might become impossible to break.

'After Chris had been in hospital, and it looked as though it would be unlikely he'd be back to work, I went through his office – you know, in preparation for the shift. Actually, I must confess, I was rather hoping I might move in – it's got a lovely view – but mainly I think it was a gesture to get closer

to him, somehow. This isn't what
you're asking, I'm afraid. Yes, there
was a small box, a shoebox, of
pornography – magazines, that sort
of thing – in one of the cupboards.
I brought it home before the clean-
ers or the secretary discovered it.'

'Do you still have it?'

'Yes.'

'I'd like it,' I said.

'Of course,' he replied, then
paused. 'What, *now*?'

'If it's possible.'

He returned some minutes later.
The sides of the box, I noticed, had
been reinforced at some stage with
packing tape. He placed it on the
edge of the cane table.

'I'm sorry, Sorel,' he said.

'What for?' I asked.

'I should never have sent the
manuscript. I just assumed . . . I
suppose it was a fairly stupid
assumption.'

'Not really,' I replied.

I moved from the lounge into the
hallway, and as I turned back, my

eyes met those of this strange woman whose appearance was so similar to mine. Our eyes met briefly, then we re-entered our respective worlds, moving from each other at this quite unnatural speed.

The night of our return from Paris, the furniture, in the light that issued palely from the hallway lamp, seemed to be drifting in the room. It was how I'd remembered these pieces, coming to my mother's house that final time: the faint notes of lavender, and the armchairs beneath their sheets, gently knocking at the edges of the room.

All these faces. These brutal and these sad appropriations. I lifted them from the box, not wishing to touch them but for this awful necessity.

If this were his choice, I thought,

if he had chosen this way – turning to them, page after page – it must have always been his choice.

I'd come in search of Catherine and found her everywhere. I found her limbs pulled wide apart by metal bars. I found her hung by ropes. I found her screaming, impaled upon an arm. Her mouths agape. I found these endless deaths by drowning.

Grief. Release. Anger. Numbness. I took her photograph and held it to my face. She is offering her life for you. Here she is. Here she is. I am yours, she says. We hear her say.

I should have mentioned it before, but I have had this dream. For weeks now. It is winter, not as it was on that perfect, hot, December day. What happens does so as if it were months ago.

Nor, at the start, does it appear that I am really myself so much as a passer-by, coming upon the scene by chance.

It is a cold September morning. There is rain. A semi-frozen rain. A drizzle whose slowness is akin to snow. There is a car, a Renault 12, beside a kerb. The road is Blackburn Road (but that is not correct outside the dream) in Clayton, near where the drive-in used to be. It appears to be quite poorly parked: the front wheels pointed at, rather than beside, the kerb. The windows have misted in the cold, caused by the interior's only trace of life: a raucous breathing.

I turned the bookmark, placed it horizontally upon the desk. The back of the red-brown card unmarked except by this address.

I wrote, frightened that this mightn't be an ending so much as another beginning, that perhaps it might be simpler to live with doubt. I wrote as much with the fear of exhaustion as with the fear of embarrassment. As much the fear of lucidity as the fear of failure.

East Melbourne
February 1

Dear Frances Bourin,

You will recall we met at a dinner party held by Kate Metherall in late May of last year.

I believe that you and my husband Christopher corresponded after our return to Australia, that it was an intimate correspondence involving an emotional commitment of some intensity.

I say, 'believe.' I myself have no specific proof apart from a manuscript of Christopher's which indicates this is the case, and the testimony of an acquaintance which suggests the existence, but not the substance, of these letters.

I have no wish to pursue this

beyond simple verification and to offer, obviously, my sincere apologies should this not be the case.

You will not know, but Christopher suffered a stroke recently – ironically, perhaps, precipitating the events leading to this letter. It is not expected that he will recover and no one can be sure exactly how long he will live, though it is felt more than a month may be optimistic.

Although I cannot expect it, I would appreciate a reply, or some acknowledgment of this letter.

Yours faithfully,
Sorel Atherton

Despite the mist there could be seen, at the front driver-side of the car, a pale blot of flesh pressed against the glass.

From inside I could hear the stertorous, saliva-ridden breathing, half-snore, half-snort. I crouched down to get closer to the window. I could make out a body slumped against the door, head turned to the right, resting against the glass. And this face, once so familiar to me, slowly dawning on me, as it were: asymmetrical, slightly frozen.

Then, quite unexpectedly, I came across the photograph of the woman with the two men. Her biography was there, as the manuscript had mentioned – only Christopher had corrected a typographical error in the French (which gave *état* instead of *était*) and changed the name Ronny to Georges.

I have no reasonable explanation for this latter change. Georges was Catherine's accomplice, but this seems quite gratuitous. Perhaps he felt Ronny to be as real as any of us, and in need of some disguise?

His face seemed succulent: pale

fruit, half eaten. What did Rilke say? That it had no more substance than a broken fruit corrupting in the air? The dying poet.

I caught a reflection in the glass of the window. Only the light things could be seen. The hair was not visible. The face, yes. Its pallor. The whiteness of the face, white as Christopher's pale face, could be seen. The material of her dress too dark. But the light-glint from the buttons and the single brooch was visible, as was the whiteness of her clenched hands.

'I read your book. About a week ago. I haven't mentioned it because I was unsure of what to say. Perhaps it is beautiful – I'm not sure of that either. I'm blinded by the facts, so faithfully recorded, of those final months. By your articulation of my loss, and your hatred, and the stupidity of every evening. I'm so numbed, remembering, I can't tell you if the descriptions, of themselves, constitute a thing of beauty.

'Christopher, that's not why I am here . . . '

I stared at his absolutely silent face, the eyes roving aimlessly across the room. Perhaps if I had been totally convinced that he could hear what I was saying, I might have carried through these final meetings in a mutual silence. I shall never know.

'I've written to Frances.'

What if she had never written back? For it would seem far too benign of life for her to have replied expressing incredulity, if not offence. What if that reply had never come from France? I'm not sure which would have been worse: the confirmation or the remaining doubt. With one there is the pain of his deceit, but also clarity; with the other, the pain of my own sense of betrayal.

I doubted him.

Paris
February 12

Dear Sorel Atherton,

So he is to die.
Please accept my sympathy for your present grief and for that greater grief to come – which is mine also, and deeply so.

I shall make no secret of the fact that I cried at this news. It should have made no difference. Everything is without shame, without guilt, but with a regret. Poor Christopher.

I doubt you will wish a long letter from me. However, let me say there was the temptation (for simplicity, if nothing else) to lie, or simpler still, to leave your letter unanswered. Yes, we wrote to each other – what you have gathered from your enquiries is true.

As to the actual substance of our 'affair', it is more difficult to weigh. As I once wrote to Christopher, had we both still been living in Paris (or

Melbourne), there is no doubt we would have followed through with this relationship. You must judge me then as you might judge an ordinary mistress.

I believe though that what I have done would be wrong only if I had done it with a sense of wrong. Or fear. But I have no fear. I take it upon myself. What I have written, I have written quite wilfully and consciously. It was important for me, as I believe it was for him. There was a splendid difference about the whole exchange. An insanity which was beguiling and arousing. Yes. You see, I am tired of sense. It is sense that has already passed its judgment on me.

Sometimes I wonder if I am the last of this generation (my God, I am nearly fifty – my daughter has now taken lovers) for whom sex is this unfulfillable imperative.

To be condemned by the irrational was a far more privileged fear. For this I owe Christopher an apology. I had ascribed the sudden termination of his correspondence to some timidity. I challenged him with this – I retain a copy of my more important correspondence – I asked him, 'Did I frighten you off with my last letter? I would never have thought that possible. And ours was just a mental thing, it was just correspondence. What if it had been real?' No, I could not believe it of him. Indeed, your letter has explained his silence, and these accusations tell me more, now, of myself than of him.

Presumably, my final letter must still be at his Hawthorn studio. If this is so, perhaps you might arrange for it to be destroyed. It is clearly based upon a quite inaccurate assumption, and is no proper epitaph.

As for his manuscript, this was something he did not mention to me. Has he turned me into fiction, I wonder? It would be interesting, I suppose, to see what he has conjured from our brief exchange. You see, I loved his writing.

Yours sincerely,
Frances Bourin

This vile mind, so oozy, so hypocritical, praise-mad, canting, envious, concupiscent!

※ 3 ※

I'm not sure if this is all too obvious, or whether none of it makes sense other than to me, who now knows everything. It's just that far too much has come to pass, and everything depends on every other thing for its meaning. Let me try and clarify at least something here: every word of this novella *happened*, and my own arrival at that understanding was terrible, and full of pain.

At what point do you cease knowing someone? Or perhaps the question is at what point do you begin. It terrified me to realise that whilst our lives had maintained their apparent continuities, whilst the surfaces remained undisturbed, Christopher had been living in this other world.

Suddenly it seemed most likely that I'd never known this man, that he'd always kept the dark centre of himself unilluminated, that the real energy of his life had burned in these desires. It seemed too that if he hadn't actually brought himself to lie, he must have chosen words which would not compromise this separate existence. A clever, crafted language.

But if these words had meant these other things, couldn't they have meant them from the very first moment of their use?

Mightn't the words that he spoke to me once, in love, be nothing more than script? I recalled the silences of our final years, now so obviously filled with resentment at my presence, a situation from which he found it impossible to break free. This man, so much wishing to suffer, so much seeking plausible reason why the world he desired had not materialised, needing the excuse to stop himself from finding out it could never exist.

We grieve, we anger, we despair. Then there is this long, barely endurable emptiness.

He said he loved me.

'She sent the letters *here*. She told me, to his "Hawthorn studio"! It wasn't a suspicion that you had. You knew about it, didn't you!'

His face, I can remember, went

through a welter of expressions: at first an almost naïve hopefulness, an infant joy at my arrival, itself flickering almost instantly into apprehension; then, after my words were spoken, the look of a discovered child. Yet finally – and this is far more difficult to put in words – there was the relief of some nervous player whose moment had arrived at last.

I wasn't sure I wanted to continue this. I knew the truth, if not the details, and my visit to Jeremy's house was in one sense nothing more than a means of confronting him with my awareness of his complicity, of telling him I knew he'd lied. But this had all been achieved in the semi-darkness of his porch.

Now I realise that by entering I was grasping for a final chance, the slightest hope that Jeremy would have some additional piece of information which might restore the balances, bring equilibrium to this chaotic world. I entered then out of that hope which is the admission of despair.

The room was silent – its walls' charcoal and slate a darkening underbelly of cloud – the silence of the storm's still heart.

He had begun.

'Chris came to me, late June, I think it was – *quite* late – and asked if it were possible to use my address for some correspondence. He told me that he'd met a woman in Paris, shortly before he'd left, and wanted to remain in contact, that it might be simpler all around if you didn't know about it. In case you got the wrong idea. I wasn't sure how I could refuse. I mean, to say no, was tantamount to saying I suspected him of an affair.'

'Do you have the letters here?' The disgusting thought breaking suddenly upon me. 'Have you *read* them?'

'No, of course not – to both.

When a letter arrived I'd bring it in to work . . . '

'And he'd never talk about it?'

'Sorel, God. A little, yes. Only in the most general terms – what I told you last time, that it had become increasingly erotic.'

'So when he presented you with the manuscript, you knew *exactly* what it was, of what it was made.'

His body first moved forward, then, as it had the evening of our previous meeting, collapsed back in the armchair: a marionette whose strings had been severed by my words.

'Yes.'

What is love to a man?

It is one of the riddles that this body asks me. This body hovering in the mist, anus raised high like a cat, whose limbs taper to their hooves, whose wings have not feathers but (worse than scales) flints! Whose head is a mass of

157

baby's curls.

When a man declares his love, what does he mean?

What is this afterburn I cannot erase, holding me to this disfigured body? Who is this man who angers me? Not because of these acts – these saddening and pathetic acts, these acts of self-doubt – but because of this waste of time. Because of what he has done to everything which might have been of value.

I forgot myself. I told him I knew that he'd lied to me. Deserted me. Betrayed me. That he was quite shameless and disgusting. I told him he was weak, pathetically weak.

I think now that I must have endlessly repeated myself, because when I try to recall my words I find a memory of the same thing said again, but slightly differently.

I said that what he had achieved was to render everything he'd ever said a lie. I said, 'You are going to leave me, now, with everything you ever said or did a lie.'

I remember walking around the bed, back and forth, gathering myself, composing myself.

'I'm tired of being deserted. I'm tired of having to come to terms with the weakness of others – of supporting them, of giving every-thing to them, so they can leave.

'The other evening, lying in bed, I thought of that myth, with the young girl following her poet . . .

'I had died, and somehow you'd brought me back to life, those final weeks. I thought there might be hope (I was unsure of love, if I could ever look at you as once I must have looked) because you came to me, Christopher; you told me you were sorry. You said you loved me.

'Then your book began to turn. Your book began to stare at me . . . and I suddenly died a second time. *Christopher, to die again is a shocking thing!* Not only do you find yourself exhausted from that ceaseless holding back of doubt, the cost of this other life is *hope*: each hour persuading you to surrender more and more of your defences.

'Then all at once you realise that everything has come back to the same familiar point, that all this effort – doing everything this second time – has been for nothing. And there is the sense of waste, doubled; the pointlessness, doubled; the doubled pain of every wound reopening.'

I paused. What needed to be said had lost its logic; the thoughts no longer followed naturally one from the other. I didn't know – because there were so many things, or because the circumstances were so strange, so rife with ambiguity – where I might begin. I said a type of aphorism.

'Faithfulness is only respect. Your crime is the *existence* of these fantasies.'

Inside my head, I heard his loud

objection, knowing him (at least in this regard) so well.

'It *is* fair, Christopher. I know what you would say: "I never touched her. It was an intellectual exercise." Too well. No, Jesus of Nazareth was right: you have looked upon this woman with lust, and it *is* enough.

'It was the way I saw you look at every woman, every day – like you were perusing fruit. Choosing, finding blemish, choosing once again.

'I'd rather it had finished six months ago, a year ago – and yes, I'll say it , just as you did – *seven* years ago. Whenever it might have been that you first started living out these vicarious lives as opposed to what it was you chose to offer me. But to suggest it might be love – small, small, small.'

I have seen it, time and time again, in the few men who have entered my life, mostly in the lives of my closest friends: Beth, Carola, Lotte, Merry, Deborah, each of their lives a type of psalm, a version of lament: To whose beds their husbands have returned, their breath, their hands, their penises odoured with the trace of other women, quite enlivened! As possibly once they may have carried our scents back to others.

For what of those who have been deserted because we have been the chosen ones? We who had consented to these betrayals, if only from the belief that we should be loved again. Perhaps our sole excuse is here: that afterwards we had continued loving. We had put our faith in these relationships and hadn't thought we should protect ourselves.

Men are quite without faith. No, this is not fully true: they have faith, only for them it appears a fragile thing. A thing which dies.

It comes to you how every call could be *that* call, the ringing interrupting you from other interruptions, the voice upon you before you have the time to make an adequate defence. The serious voice conveying its authority and right to speak, suspicious of the awkward or irrational response.

'Do you know where they are?'

'The letters? Not here. Not at the office. I assume you've checked his study and such. I imagine he destroyed them.'

'What about the final letter?'

I saw his eyes dart back and forth, the one, it seemed, slightly slower than the other. Damaged.

'In what sense, final? I'm sorry, I'm not quite sure what you mean.'

Whatever vulnerability I may have momentarily unearthed was shored up by his question and the time that it had taken him to ask.

'Frances told me that she'd

written a letter to which there'd been no reply. I wondered if that letter might be here.'

'The final letter. Yes, I see. Well, it arrived a month or so after the previous one. I hung on to it naturally, for a while, and then when it was obvious he wasn't going to recover, I destroyed it. Threw it out.'

I couldn't stop myself replying.

'So the three of you kept your secret to the end.'

'Was it possible to tell you? Sorel, look at it from the position I was in. Christopher was my friend. I'd agreed to act as go-between long before I realised the import of it all.'

'But when you found out what it was that you were doing, then you could have gone to him and told him no.'

Even before he spoke, I realised what I'd done. How I'd made it possible for him to say these things, my speech a prompt for everything he wished released.

If you like, quite inadvertently I had spoken the magic words that had unloosed a demon.

'I couldn't have done that, Sorel. You see, I wanted him to leave you.'

I heard. It was impossible to avoid his horrible unburdening.

'He didn't want you any more; his mind was full of *her*.'

I stood to leave. But he continued with this speech, his voice becoming louder and louder, shouting as I moved away.

'I love you, Sorel, I have loved you more than seven years . . . '

At the time I made a set of notes to which I have returned: for the purpose of sharing, for the purpose of comparison. I remember calling them The Days of Waves, because over that time it seemed I had been lying on a distant shore and that these things had broken over me, quite beyond my control, like vast waves.

THE DAYS OF WAVES

This is the first day: helplessness. The feeling of moving as in a dream. Numbness. A forgetting that one is walking. A lack of concern at walking with such forgetfulness.

...

The loss of one's vocabulary in the midst of speaking. An inability to articulate. A lack of concern at, a giving in to, inarticulateness. A surrender to the inarticulate. A falling, yes, it seems literally, into silence.

...

Tiredness. The feeling of having just completed a journey of great length, but with no sense of arrival, merely of being somewhere else that must be left.

...

The fear that one might never sleep. The eating of meals out of obligation, without hunger. Hearing oneself (a mother) saying, you must eat, or you'll be ill . . .

....

A desire to seek photographs, letters, and a fear of doing so for what it might unleash. A need to verify appearances.

...

Forgetfulness. Vagueness. A drifting off. An inability to finish and a lack of caring that a thing be finished. A subduedness in speech. A sudden hearing of one's own occasional loudness and distaste at such a lapse.

...

Wandering. The necessity for wandering.

...

A sudden fierce devotion to the child. To the small fists raised in their struggle. Finding oneself staring at this unknown child, talking to its mother, as though one had been related to them in some direct lineage by death. A realisation of the preciousness of the child, worthy of our adoration. Granting us serenity in chaos. Fierceness against apathy. Selah.

...

Physical things. The jaw aching through certain necessary holdings-back of tears.

With the tears: that aching of the neck
and shoulders, the discomfort in the chest.
A sense that everything inside one has
shrunk and is pulling at the outer flesh.

...

Then nothing. Only the eyes' afterburn.
A consciousness of breathing, like the
beginning of a cold rather than a simple
consequence of this death.

...

Days of impatience. An irritation at the
slightest demand that might be placed
on one. Then anger. The frustrated
anger of a child.

...

The noticing. How many ordinary
objects were saturated in this person.
How one is surprised. Resonances.
Everything that might connect: not only
mention of the obvious words – the
name, the relationship – but sounds, a
furniture, a perfume (like the sudden
shock of lavender). Everything in meta-
phoric connection. Returning like persistent refrains. Grief is a type of poetry.

...

Closing the gate and glimpsing back, I clutched at my stomach. His final words, half heard as I pulled the door on them, had sickened me. I shuddered at the momentary thought that a desire sufficiently intense might somehow be transmitted by sheer force of will, that the violation of his words might somehow grow within me.

As I reached the car I heard the whisking of the bushes from outside his porch, cosseting their mania of darkness, possessed, enthralled – about to speak in tongues. Then finally, that long, quite horrible cry.

This sound – an almost animal howl of pain – might possibly have been the echo of myself, except I knew that I had kept my silence. It was, I must suppose, from Jeremy. From whom I had just walked away, still numbed beyond the slightest possibility of sympathy. For even now, I couldn't bring myself to believe that it was over.

The telephone again, like some small child's voice demanding to be answered. Our lives perpetually disturbed. Our meditations scattered.

When they pulled the curtains round my mother (here, where he had finally deserted her, this second time), it seemed not so much a gesture of theatricality as something quite domestic. Something I had seen her do each night, a thousand times.

It was as though she had become the 'outside world' which they had seen grow dark, grow threatening – and they wished to turn the lights on in this living place. Yes, she was dark and she was cold. So they drew the curtains on her. Kept her out.

The call was from a nurse.

'It looks as if your husband may've had another bleed.'

He was to die.

I drove out to the hospital. I remember thinking that it would coincide with visiting hour. That parking would be difficult. I remember it was raining heavily. One of those relentless, idiotic, turn-of-season Melbourne rains that quite forgets to stop, or seems incapable of stopping.

It comes as no surprise it is my father's face against the misted glass – I had expected it – the full expressions somehow unstitched, and pulled apart.

'I must come to see you,' he is saying, 'even if it's only for an hour.' His voice sounds old. It frightens me that age should be so ludicrous on him. 'I need to talk to you.'

I think, He comes to me, a father, when I no longer need a father.

'We don't have to lie to one another any more,' I say. 'I'm not a child. I can't believe your stories any more.'

I think, I tried so long to win him back. I sang for him. To tempt him home. I was a siren for him.

'Go on!' I hear him screaming through the glass. 'Tell me that I'll never come to anything. Tell me I am beyond love. Tell me that I'm self-absorbed . . . Everything your mother used to tell me.'

'She's dead,' I cry into the telephone. 'While you were gone. Now keep away!'

I was sitting at a table in the cafeteria – almost precisely where I'd been seated whilst waiting for Christopher to be taken to his room – amidst a noise sharpened by hard surfaces: the chrome benches and the troughs, the glass racks and displays. A clockface reading 8.15.

I'd been searching for her. Trying to catch a glimpse of this woman somewhere in the room. There she was! Distorted, interrupted by the shifting queue, but there, in the thick glass of the servery.

I watched her rising slowly from the table. Her pot of tea, like mine, left untouched.

Then for a moment she was lost to view, reappearing quite clearly though as she approached the glass door of the exit. She was reaching for the very handle, when suddenly she sheared off, flattened, thinned, distorted, like some ghost taking flight at the living. She was gone. Behind me there was hubbub in the foyer. There were many strangers carrying flowers.

I'd already forgotten how the weather had been at the time of my arrival. I stared down at my own body: at my own arms and at the cone of my coat; at the distant brown shoes, too small it seemed to carry all that loomed above them, too small it seemed to retain the balance that they did.

A man appeared in front of me.

He had been holding back the
door. He had stepped aside to
let me pass. I felt his eyes upon
me, seeking once again to jettison
me into death.

I strode outside. My hands pushing through the threads of rain held
out like bribes within the passing
lights.

AFTERWORD

I have been looking over everything
that we have written. No doubt
you'll think I have been dwelling on
this – in one sense, yes – but the
grief is of a different order.

It seems strange after the magni-
tude of these events that minor
details should obsess me so. I have
no wish to tell them all, but they are
of this order: of wondering why it
was that Christopher had waited to
reply to Frances's letter of

December 3.

There would have been a week. Perhaps, by then, he could sustain himself in fantasy alone? It's difficult to say and, without his letters, quite impossible to know.

Another thing, almost, I suppose, stylistic. Carola, who'd spent a week in Paris recently and sought to visit Le Rubis, only to find it closed the month of August (with whom I've shared the manuscript, and no less, my pain), had pointed out this small discrepancy in the beginning of the letter dated August 3.

Of course, you say, the evocation is poetic, and there's no reason after all why Frances shouldn't have sought to intensify the feeling of romance in her writing at this time.

Maybe just these trivialities, now, are all I wish to know.

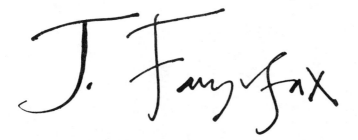

JEREMY FAYRFAX

❈ THE VIRGIN ❈

It was as if I had awoken from a dream to find myself awry: my posture crooked, quite half cocked, my neck exposed, my head thrown backwards like a baying wolf.

From outside came the 'clop' of the gate's metal latch, almost liquid in its sound: a word pronounced by some watering mouth. Then the turning over of the engine cutting through the swirling blackness, a volley of dog bark, *ra-ra-ra-ra-ra*, and she had gone, leaving me, halted mid-room in my shock.

Yes, as if awakening, I began to reassemble fragments, piecing back together the preceding moments. How, for instance, the last part of my speech must have been unheard (I have the recollection of her moving from the room), and spoken, for example, to the mantelpiece.

'Sorel, you're the only woman I've ever met I could imagine carrying my child.' Spoken ludicrously out loud towards the empty hall. 'I can imagine your devotion, fiercely radiant.'

No more than this. Only a sudden pause at the realisation of my own words (their noise within the room), then nothing – more like fit than dream – until I heard the gate, until I heard the hollow door-slam and the turning of the engine.

Perhaps her exit had allowed some of the night to permeate the room, for it had darkened. It was possible now to detect shadows amongst the folds of curtaining, in the fabrics of the armchairs. There, beneath the mantelpiece! A pervasive chiaroscuro beginning to assert itself within this space.

I remember thinking that the curtains had been drawn against the heat of a late-January day – a single *tranche* of light coming from the window, its beam aswarm with particles of dust – then realising, no, the curtains had been drawn because of their departure.

I found myself to be trembling in a state of anticipation, scarcely less than sexual. You see, I was to be 'in charge', I was to 'stay here every once in a while' – Christopher had said these things to me.

'Jeremy, while we're away in Paris, would you be prepared to look after the house? Collect any stray mail, that sort of thing?'

He had given me the key. He had unloosed me in the heart of this

place: here, amongst the endless
traces of her presence. These places
where she slept, and where she
cleansed herself, where she squat-
ted, ridding her body of its wastes.
He had granted me the feel, the
odour and the taste of these objects
with which she surrounded herself,
that previously I had only glimpsed.
He had given me this tabernacle for
my use, until the time of their
return.

Over the days I began to imagine
it as the place where I would
eventually live with her, to the
extent that, on certain evenings, I
would take the journey from Hawthorn to East Melbourne to rehearse
our moments together. I would call
to her from a distant room, imagining her voice in reply – but only if
he were to leave. Only if that
dissatisfaction which I understood
within him were to grow; if some
yearning might carry him outside his
fear, outside the shadow of his guilt.

In such a reverie, I had quite

forgotten my own presence in their house, rediscovering myself, as it were, only by the dull drum of my blood, the high nerve-whine; by my breath, a slowly breaking wave.

I flicked on the light and looked about me, catching my image in the dressing-table's oval mirror. Fayrfax in his thirty-seventh year, I thought. A trace of grey that strokes amongst the pale brown curls of hair, or from the gingered beard. A single coin of unsilvered glass, oil-bright, blemishing his face.

In the corner of the room stood a large keyless wardrobe, its russet wood radiating a soft luminance. I stared at its brown-black door and it seemed I heard, from the depths of the gaping lock, a distant sound: some vague and joyous murmur.

I slowly pulled the bottom drawer – releasing to the air a note of lavender, sharp and ineradicable – moving upwards on the left-hand side: through the gloves and scarves and straps, the shed skins of stockings, a medicated cream, a box of tampons, a single brassière – flesh-toned and prophylactic. Then down: the underwear, the silk and nylon crackling, catching at the rough sides of my fingers . . .

Christopher was in the open doorway. Sheepish, suddenly quite so adolescent I might have mistaken his posture for that of an undergraduate seeking an extension for his essay.

'Jeremy, could I have a word?' I think he said, with ridiculous formality. Obviously enough, he had rehearsed it. Entering the office he pulled to the door, pausing halfway to ask, 'Do you mind?'

I nodded in the direction of the leather chair. The next pause was excruciatingly long.

'I was wondering if I might ask a favour.' It was awkward for him, so much so as to enliven me with its potential. I remember my mouth filling with saliva.

He began picking at the raised seam of the chair, its noise amongst his sentences like punctuation.

'You might recall, about a month before we left Paris I went to a reading at the Village Voice Bookshop. I would have mentioned it in a letter . . . '

'Yes.' I could recall. Kate Metherall had been there, accompanied, more significantly it had appeared, by an older woman, finely boned, with deep red hair. The letter had dwelt a trifle long on her, enough to suggest he might wish to write of nothing else – too much of her opinion of *A Sport and a Pastime*. A question of proportion, where the description of a single gesture, a single attribute of appearance, might disturb a sense of natural balance, might topple everything from anecdote into confession.

'I met a woman there. Frances Bourin. Do you recall?'

'I think so, yes.'

He picked.

'I remember it occurring to me at the time that she was a sort of kindred spirit, and she said that we *must* keep in touch.'

He stopped, his sentence hanging with its slightly upward inflection. Perhaps he hoped he had said enough, that I would finish off what needed to be said or asked and then quietly accede.

'I'd like to write to her, of course. Except that it might prove a little awkward – I mean, should it become a regular correspondence – with the letters coming to East Melbourne. And to use the university's address says far too obviously, Write to me at work. You see the problem. And then I thought, if I were to use your address, as if it were my own, I mean . . . '

He was a boy engaged in his first misdemeanour, barely capable of holding back a nervous laugh. I think, had not this action the potential to destroy his marriage, it would have quite disgusted me.

'I was thinking,' he continued, 'I might ask her to write to my "Hawthorn studio".'

He was to be unfaithful. And there begins my story, I suppose, in earnest. He no longer loved Sorel. This subterfuge was, at least, his first admission of the fact – as later he would hint at and agonise his way through our afternoon confessions. Yes, above all else, it seems in retrospect, he wanted to confess. Remember that.

The first of my eleven o'clock class had come tapping at the door.

I acquiesced. I yelled, 'Come in,' so that there would be no more of it. In order that the business be completed. The arrangement sealed. 'After all,' I added, 'I would hate for you to "lose touch".'

It was Sorel who had knocked, standing in the ochrish glow of the porch light. I knew almost instantly what had happened. Just as a voice across a telephone imparts tragedy well before the first sentence has been completed, I had this split-second of realisation before her words burst over me.

'I wrote to Frances. She sent her letters here, to his "Hawthorn studio", didn't she! It wasn't a suspicion that you had; you knew about it from the start.' Behind her, there seemed a wild cavort of plants, a tarantella, both of uncontrol and ecstasy.

I had never expected Sorel to write to Frances, if only because the address would be unknown, kept from her by Christopher. I was, for a moment, quite unmanned at her discovery. Then I began to see in this a possibility to say what I had wanted said for many years. Furthermore, I felt the very extremity of my action, the depth of passion it revealed, might well eventually recommend me, in her eyes.

I asked her to come in then, not out of fear, but with relief, and with joy at a rich opportunity. Without this incident, how long might I have harboured my unspoken love, how long before the circumstance arose in which I had no choice but this admission.

I recall her, perched at the very edge of the settee, leaning forward, her right leg outstretched, the left folded back beneath her thigh: her whole body in precarious balance, demanding explanation.

I began by telling her all I have already mentioned: how Christopher had asked if he might use my address, how he had met a woman in Paris and wished to correspond with her.

'He said everything might be simpler if you didn't know about it,' I continued. 'In case you got the wrong idea.

'I wasn't sure how I could refuse. After all, to say no, suggested I suspected him of an affair.'

She asked me if I knew the letters' whereabouts, and of course

I had to tell her no.

It wasn't easy for Sorel. I felt the desperation underpinning her anger. Hers was a vulnerable indignation, and one which might be turned.

It was then she posed a question for which I had been unprepared. She asked about the final letter.

Of course, with what she knew, she could only have meant one thing by this enquiry. And all I needed then was to steady myself and exercise a simple rigorous logic. I told her that one other had arrived perhaps a month or so after Frances's previous correspondence. That I had retained it, against all likelihood that Christopher would actually read it. And finally, that I had thrown it out, unopened.

At this, she became quite accusatory.

'So the three of you kept your secret to the end.'

I, of course, could only point out that I had no other choice. I had agreed to a friend's request, in all good faith, and quite without the knowledge of what would eventuate.

'But when you found out what it was that you were doing,' I heard her voice come in reply, 'then you could have gone to him and told him no.'

They were perfect words. It was as if I had been forced into my speech, *compelled* to make this utterance I had dreamed of making year after year.

'No, I couldn't,' I could suddenly explain. 'Because I wanted him to leave you.' And I paused, quite free now of responsibility for everything I said. 'Because I love you, Sorel. I have loved you now for over seven years.'

I was standing in the room. It hardly mattered where. Perhaps another fifteen minutes had elapsed. The wind had fiercened. Now each sound of that outside world arrived distorted in some extreme pianoforte, by turns too close, too far.

She had gone, but I knew she had already heard enough. She had heard this declaration of my love. I had sowed the seed of this knowledge within her. It was my hope, where before, in silence, there was hopelessness.

I moved the telephone closer to my chair. I poured a glass of wine. I considered tidying the room, but, should she choose to return that evening, things would need to appear as they were when she had left. I did, however, take the precaution of inspecting the bed, and made it up in a relaxed, informal manner.

I waited. Quickening at the approach of every car, anticipating the slowing down, the cricking of the handbrake, the door-slam, the metallic drop which is the opening of the gate: everything which would lead to that final half-rap at the door, distorted by this dervish wind, each noise covering me, uncovering me with its waves.

I seemed to have awoken yet again, my legs crossed, my left leg quite numbed. I lifted its dead weight to the floor, waiting for the prickling to emerge, and to subside. Two o'clock. I raised myself out of the chair and hobbled to the bedroom. I sat on the edge of the bed and reached for the wooden box upon the bedside table. Holding back its lid, I withdrew the postcard reproduction of Leonardo's *The Virgin, Child and Saint Anne*.

I gazed at these three figures, locked together in their passion, my eyes following down the Virgin's body (this slightly breasted, pale-nippled body as I had imagined it), resting at the fulcrum point, and back then to her face, the hair scarved, pulled from the forehead, the eyes cast down.

I should tell you now what I had tried to tell Sorel, shouting, at the time of her departure: that I wished her pregnant, when I had never before wished this with any woman. I wished to see the absolute radiance of that face illuminate my child.

But what I have never told – this secret I keep close, unspoken – is the peculiar wonder that the painting has for me. How I knew this face, from the moment of recognition, cutting its swathe of silence through that relentless traffic of the gallery; how it swam back to me, though at that time we were half the world apart. And I had never told her this.

It is a simple thing, this love I have for the work, why I have, over the years (from the time indeed when I first saw the painting and realised the strange coincidence!), dwelt upon it. Perhaps overly? It is this. It is because the face of the Virgin is Sorel's face. Exactly. It might as well be a photograph.

And with the picture of it, I lay back upon the counterpane, and wept.

THE VIRGIN, CHILD AND
✽ SAINT ANNE ✽

(AN ESSAY)

'It seemed to me that as I lay in my cradle, a vulture came to me; opening my mouth, and striking me several times between my lips, with its tail.'

So Freud quoted from one of Leonardo's earliest childhood recollections. It is a startling fantasy. And the central question it raises appears as intriguing now as it most certainly must have been to Freud: why has the suckling mother been replaced by a vulture?

'At such a point,' considered Freud, 'a thought comes to mind from so remote a quarter that it would be tempting to set it aside. In the hieroglyphics of the ancient Egyptians, the mother is represented by a picture of a vulture. The Egyptians also worshipped a Mother

Goddess, who was represented as having a vulture's head, or else several heads, of which at least one was a vulture's. This goddess's name was pronounced *Mut*. Can the similarity to the sound of our word *Mutter* be merely a coincidence?'

So, in his 1910 essay, *Leonardo da Vinci and a Memory of His Childhood*, Freud was able to associate the mother, approaching with her imagined erect penis, with the androgynous vulture-headed goddess, *Mut*, and through this argue a case for the artist's passive homosexuality.

By way of seeming confirmation, some three years later the analyst Oskar Pfister discovered, as a type of 'unconscious picture-puzzle', the actual outline of a vulture in the blue-grey cloth of Mary's drapery in Leonardo's painting, *The Virgin, Child and Saint Anne*.

Needless to say, all of this strikes us as absurd, if for no other reason than that the initial association is based on Freud's mistranslation of *nibbio* as 'vulture', and not as 'kite'.

The painting in question hangs in the Denon wing of the Louvre museum. Though only metres from the *Mona Lisa*, surrounded by its constantly replenishing crowds, all trace of clamour has abated. It is as if this trinity of figures has silenced them, reduced their ragged babble to mere distant murmurings. Instead, one is enraptured by an absolute serenity; overwhelmed by this painting's sense of flow, the sweep of the diagonals, a movement which has begun in the very landscape: the curve and fall of the river. Or is it mist?

Why are they here, these women and this child, perched at the precipice edge, these generations linked together in the softest chain of flesh?

Much discussion of the painting has centred on the half-completed action of the Virgin: the mother's desire to draw her Son back from

His wilful embrace of self-sacrifice. Yet even the most perfunctory inspection dispels any suggestion of concern upon her face. There is no sense of competing emotions here – rather there is a calm acceptance. The Virgin is captured at the moment of action. As for Saint Anne, she appears no more than a dispassionate observer.

But this has not always been the case.

In particular, I am interested in the last occasion on which they 'met', as it were, for any length of time.

For this we must return to a charcoal drawing, *The Virgin and Child with Saint Anne and the Infant Saint John*, dating from some four years previously.

To look upon this earlier cartoon is to refer almost to a prior conversation, a glimpse of a moment in which, it would seem, advice is given and a decision made. Visually, the Virgin and Saint Anne are of the same age, the drawing suggesting the women to be sisters or friends, rather than mother and daughter. Furthermore, their decision is undeniably carnal: their faces could be seamlessly collaged into a porno-graphic image. (And should this seem extreme, does not one of the more worrisome picture-puzzles that insinuate themselves amongst the painter's later work here include the erect phallus? Does not the left hand of the Virgin cup the testicles of this hidden member?) How earthbound they appear, for they have yet to don the masks of radiance and serenity.

In particular, Saint Anne appears to be suggesting some action or opinion, conspiratorial in its nature. She has already turned half into the shadow; the darkness almost, but not totally, obscuring the slight disfigurement of her right eye. *Her* mouth holds none of the enigma characteristic of other Leonardo women: the smile is tempting, sinister, collusive, and the Virgin has quite clearly treated Anne's suggestion with favour, her head tilted in attention, a corresponding smile about to break upon her lips. The umbrous visage of Saint Anne! 'Wounded in the eye, a mask upon her face of fair appearance, whilst making a contemptuous motion towards Heaven.'

This apposite description is, in fact, from Leonardo: an earlier observation entitled 'Envy'. Equally apposite might be his note upon the kite that 'when it sees its young ones growing too big in the nest, *out of envy*, it pecks their sides, and keeps them without food . . . ' And this from the man who felt that 'to write thus clearly of the kite would seem to be my destiny'. He, whose speech is that of kites. He, whose mouth was first penetrated by the kite.

The kite, the artist and Saint Anne are united in their various envies. And, *out of envy*, Anne has spoken her persuasive words – caught, almost fortuitously, in the shade of the charcoal and brown paper of a drawing.

Look again at *The Virgin, Child and Saint Anne*, that most serene of paintings. The Virgin, under the watchful eye of her mother, seems to urge the Child towards His sacrifice. Only in the knowledge of the earlier drawing would one detect that residue of satisfaction still apparent at the mouth of Saint Anne, the confidence, the amused cynicism.

How she has blinded us! This neutrality is complicity. The suggestion of sacrifice has been made. She can now sit back and observe. She, this fulcrum point on which the Virgin's action literally depends. She, whose hand (the simple pressure of which would tip one, thus balanced, quite irreversibly forward) remains concealed by the unfinished drapery, this cloak so much a work-cloth laid across some dark machine.

The Child, tipped from the precipice, entwining with the lamb, fulfils His destiny. The cloak of the Virgin rears open and a vulture shudders downwards, out of the frame's eye, chained likewise to its own imperatives.

❧ THE CHILD ❧

There was nothing then. I awoke with the first of light, the postcard semi-propped against the second pillow.

The lounge-room, its curtains drawn, lay in a preponderance of greys, objects making vague assertions of their shape against the dark. An obscure evidence of the previous hours, a history which the coming morning would slowly restore with a meticulous precision. Lightly brushing at the surfaces, the materials of the chairs; revealing who had sat most recently in which particular posture; re-establishing each minute from the char-ended cigarette butts, the fallen columns of ash, a glass three-quarters full with wine.

I waited for the telephone. For her apology at leaving as she did, and for the moment of our reconciliation.

'About last night, I'm *sorry*, Jeremy. None of this has been your fault – I realise that. There was nothing you could have done. You must forgive me. I've been under such a dreadful strain with Christopher . . . '

And so forth, till her invitation to a meal. With this difference: she would know of my love. She would know the moment she surrendered to it, how I would be hers.

For the separated lover, what is more intolerable than waiting?

The following days, my usual activity – the necessary commerce of my life – found itself replaced by thoughts of her alone, my sole desire to be with her again, this next encounter.

So began my vigil.

I could sense her everywhere within the room. This was where she left her glass that Tuesday evening (and I marked it), here her hand had rested on the mantel-piece (I stroked the coolness of the wood), here she sat upon the settee with her leg folded back beneath her. I touched the very place, resisting though the temp-tation to bend down and inhale the thick materials.

Not an hour would pass without returning to her image: I had installed a volume of Leonardo paintings, bent open at page 128, the detail of her face, upon the dresser. I carried the postcard reproduction of the entire work in my top pocket. Such are the obsessions of love!

Any interruption to these ceremonies angered me. A phone call from another was briskly terminated (perhaps she may have chosen that very moment to ring me). I blundered through the house. I became infuriated trying to find a book of Herrick I had held within my very hand, it seemed, the previous second. I cancelled the Thursday late tutorial because of the condition of my eyes, having spent several hours earlier that afternoon bathing my face in water, seeking to reduce the puffiness, the blotching of the flesh.

And then she rang.

It was to tell me Christopher had died.

'On Tuesday evening,' she related, 'about 9.00.'

I began the usual words of

sympathy, but she interrupted, thanking me, and adding there would be a small funeral on Friday afternoon.

There was not the slightest opportunity for me to say the words I had prepared during the previous week. I had failed to anticipate any of her lines or, indeed, the actual rapidity of her speech.

A funeral (and I imagined standing close behind her, watching as she bent, throwing almost matter-of-factly the handful of earth into a gaping pit) would be an awkward occasion to re-establish a relationship: the flood of memories, the presence of attentive others. It would be best to leave the thing alone for several weeks – what I had anticipated for so long could wait a little longer – and yet, the speaking of my love had instilled in me a fury of impatience.

For I knew at last how she must *have* to come to me, her radiance milking down, to give me life again.

After this proper time. After this inevitable interruption.

So, he was dead.

The Virgin, Child and Saint Anne was one of only three paintings Leonardo took with him to the Château du Clos-Lucé at Amboise in 1516. There is no reason to assume he didn't continue to work on it occasionally during his final period in France, and, given that the drapery remained unfinished, this must be considered his final painting.

Christopher said little about Amboise, either in his journal notes or in the letters he had sent to me from France, merely recording their visit to the Château, adding, in brackets, 'da Vinci models.' He appeared to have been far more taken with the dungeon at Loches, its hollow tower, the mass of pigeon-flight, a cooing like the rush of souls. Then six days later, they were at Châtel-Guyon.

Perhaps it was the metaphor of illness, perhaps the imminence of their return to Paris, but the written detail was restored by then. For several reasons it was a logical beginning.

I have of course already talked about my deep complicity in his affairs, the business of the go-between, and I cannot help but think of his request to use my address as if it were his own as the opening of some grand parenthesis, a sad digression in a life condemned to gestures of timidity, of which the following incident became the close.

It was a Tuesday, early in December, the fourth. He was in the open doorway almost exactly as he had been six months previously. Only this time he was carrying a small package.

'Can we talk?' he asked.

There was about him an air of resolve, which I came to understand to be little more than a veneer. It had taken him almost three weeks of procrastination before this firm decision, and he was without the strength, I found, to even write to Frances telling her what he had come so manfully to announce to me.

'It's over, Jeremy, the correspondence thing.'

I remember thinking I should miss our small confessional times together a day or two (religiously) after I'd passed on each letter. Never the specifics, mind, but sufficient to imply himself into a state of mild excitement.

'I've decided it's quite infantile and destructive. God, Jeremy, I've got a real relationship at home. I have to give that another chance.'

I suppose because not only are particular circumstances replicated endlessly within our own lives, but within the lives of thousands upon thousands of others, one is reduced at moments such as these to an exchange of clichés. Apart from which, what on earth could I reply?

'Are you sure it's Sorel you want to go back to?' I heard myself enquire. 'I know that sounds awfully cynical, Christopher, and I suppose I'm being the devil's advocate here, but it hasn't been good for a long time, has it? I mean, one's tempted to think of Frances as a symptom of the very problem you're now going, if you'll excuse the expression, to embrace.'

'She still loves me, Jeremy.'

I was sickened by the words. Their stupidity. I really wished this conversation over then and there, but unfortunately his speech had yet to run its course.

'I've got together everything.' He stared down at the package in his hand. 'I suppose that I should simply burn it all. But the journal's got some decent writing. Trouble is, it's full of *her* as well, you know. Look, can you keep this stuff for me? I've been carrying it around inside the briefcase now for months. It's quite ridiculous, but I can hardly leave it in the house. Not that Sorel would go through the study, you understand, but by accident . . . whatever.'

So it was that I became the guardian of the evidence of this sad *liaison*. A foolscap envelope, sealed, unmarked, delivered to me, amusingly enough, in its plain brown wrapper.

I realise that I have hardly spoken about Christopher. I might say that the analysis of character holds little interest for me. And what is there that might be said? He was an ordinary man in nearly every way. He was quick witted. He was presentable in his appearance. He was often irritatingly self-deprecating. He had a sense of some destiny unfulfilled. He *longed*. He wore leather patches on the elbows of his pullover.

Apart from this, he possessed the

thing I most desired. He had this woman and, more disgustingly, he appeared to have her love. And that was somewhat much for me to bear.

December 13 was the day on which I had Christopher deliver his completed manuscript – associating that event with the onset of his lovemaking. I have a reason for remembering it, it being the occasion when, in reality, I brought him Frances's final letter. It was unusually slight, and I presumed at the time (quite incorrectly as I was to read for myself not much more than a week later) it to be her response to his decision. It was, then, with some surprise, if not a mild disgust, that I discovered he had never bothered to reply to her previous letter of November 3. So unmanned was he, I must assume, he could not bring himself to depart with any honour, distance sparing him the indignity of flight.

If you want my opinion, the words which frightened him were

those about the necessity for making good love. I doubt his technique capable of matching his imagination, whereas she was, on her own admission, very sexually active, and fit! My God, that would have threatened him, those worrisome comparisons.

One sensed he could see the end: it was going to stop, or it would have to be pursued. For him, they were simply different types of extinction.

At the time I was not so wise; yet even so, I could hardly have expected him to welcome a further letter. No doubt he had been dreading its appearance. I, in my naïve way, had rather hoped it might upset the equilibrium that had been restored to his relationship with Sorel. A final temptation? An outburst of guilt? Something which might bring him to his senses.

In any case, we had both, it appeared, prepared our speeches: two barristers at work for prosecution and defence. Unfortunately, Christopher's, in its own piteous, self-obsessive manner, held sway.

'Jeremy,' he said, with an air of desperation when one might have reasonably expected joy, 'if this affair might ever have been possible once, it surely isn't now.'

For emphasis, it seemed to me, he sat down in the leather chair, his hands clasped between his knees. I recall he had forgotten his cigarettes and at various intervals would tap the pocket of his shirt in search of them.

'I've never told you very much about the Melbourne end of all of this, have I? And I appreciate the way you haven't asked.' He glanced up at me, briefly, on the word 'you'. Two tiny looks.

'Since Paris, actually since before that, there hasn't been a sexual relationship between us – Sorel and I. We'd walk around the house, avoiding looks. I'd spend the evenings in my study. I'd wait until she'd

gone to bed, then retire to the spare
room.

'Perhaps the letters were some
release for this. In any case they
seemed to bring me to a point of
choice: what was it that I really
wanted, emotionally and sexually,
from my life? It was as if I realised
I'd been pursuing this idea of
women for years, and that a real
person, with their own needs and
desires, had never entered into it.
The letters dragged me to the edge
of something that I'd thought I
wanted. But of course it's only from
that point, isn't it, that one can see
one doesn't really want it at all.'

After this outburst of melo-
drama, there was a pause of some
significance, in which it came to me
exactly what it was that he was
going to say. If I had been sickened
by his earlier comments on Sorel's
'love', I knew this impending declaration, with all of its attendant
carnality, would bring me close to
nausea; that is, I felt there was a

possibility I might actually be sick.

I therefore began to think about something else entirely, almost half muttering to myself beneath my breath to keep the subject matter at the forefront of my mind: an introduction I was writing for a book of poems.

> There is a staggering versatility to this language. Powerfully energetic verbs: a floor that 'thwarts', an economy that 'rises, waffles, bolts'.

His words continued relentlessly against this improvised defence, breaking through, but never wholly occupying my attention.

'After I had made my decision . . . strange hiatus in my life . . . attempt some reconciliation . . . at first we only lay beside . . . and then two days ago . . . '

I heard him say this thing. I heard him use the words 'made love'. I pictured him on top of her, for whatever quickly over moments, and I heard her tepid answering cry.

Six days afterwards he would be struck down, dumb, with no chance whatsoever of recovery. Only this uncertain time, to stare, to register God knows what of the faces that would parade about him in their half-embarrassed silences.

Paris
December 5

Dear Christopher,

What happened? Did I frighten you off with my last letter? I would never have thought that possible. All I know is that it has been a very long time since I sent it, and I have received no answer. I am beginning to believe what some men tell me – that is, that I am too *extreme*. Show me the man who is just as extreme. I am tired of the emotional cripples, the pathological liars and the cowards. I don't know

why I keep on loving men so much
when they let me down so often.
And ours was just a mental thing,
it was just correspondence. What if
it had been real?

I think I will retire to a convent,
although I can't bear the thought of
being surrounded by all those
women. Perhaps I will become a
hermit, or do what Bardot did, and
devote the second half of my life to
animals. Do you think that women
(and men) who indulge a bit too
much in sex reach saturation point?
An old friend who visited me in
Paris this week certainly has. After
a rather wild beginning, she has
given up men completely.

We are close to Christmas, and
on Friday I will be off to England
with my daughter and her boyfriend
to spend five days with my sister and
her family. Then the new year will
begin. What will it bring for you?

I hope that you will write to me
again. I enjoyed your letters so
much, and I feel as though the

momentum which was developing has been abruptly halted – a most unpleasant feeling.

Until the next time, all the best for the new year.

Frances

I placed this final letter on the pile of others, beside his Paris journal and the fledgling drafts of a novel: those worried pages which stank of labour and of the labourer. I cannot imagine at what stage he started jotting down ideas for such a venture, or, had he been capable of bringing it to a conclusion, what on earth he would have done with it! The work's *raison d'être* seemed predicated on his relationship with Frances actually coming to fruition.

None of these materials, I might add, could possibly be thought of as art – the manuscript itself was shapeless as some boned fowl – but the detail of its observation proved quite indispensable.

For Christopher and Sorel's final month in France then, I had ample material. However, from the very start I knew the seven letters from Frances would not be sufficient – perhaps under other circumstances, yes, but I was faced with the problem of his recent enlivenment, a cause for which must be attributed elsewhere.

It would be easier, I felt, to begin a sense of sexual commitment at an earlier time. (I imagined, for example, Catherine's reference to their swollen lips in letter two.) The fourth and fifth might be compounded in a single correspondence, to which I could give the date September 6. The substance of her next two letters would be perfect: the bondage was an image that I'm sure would not have occured to me, the *ménage à trois* suggesting a development so lewd, no doubt it would have frightened Christopher! It would simply now be a case of realistically filling in a sexual progression, dated at appropriate intervals which might be seen to correspond with the advent of his own preposterous coupling. And with his death.

I felt I had a month, no more. (I conceived it from the first as a tribute predicated on his still being alive at the time of its completion.)

It became expedient then to bind myself to certain self-imposed laws. It would be my practice to allow myself no mercy.

When I commenced the book, I prepared a diary, divided into weeks, and carried on for the period I had allowed myself for the completion of the work. In this I entered, day by day, the number of pages I had written, so that if at any time I had slipped into idleness for a day or two, the record of that idleness was there, staring me in the face, and demanding of me increased labour to make up the deficiency.

I would begin my writing at 5.30 every morning and continue for three hours, the first half-hour being devoted to rereading the previous day's work. The remaining time was taken up by the production of one hundred words or so, every half-hour. Indeed, I found those hundred words (a deal of which I must admit was little more than lightly edited transcription) were forthcoming as regularly as my watch went. This division of time allowed me to produce some two pages of work each day, which when kept up gave as its result a novella (as you have seen it) on January 19, this year.

I will not bore you with the finer details of the process – what was invention (augmented by my memories of Paris, and with the help of various travel guides) and what required mere transcription – suffice it to say that although many passages needed only relatively minor editing, the general application of imagination was required throughout.

To compensate, the work developed its own energy. At times it seemed I merely held the reins as Avery careered towards his destiny. Needless to say, I could not help but picture Christopher throughout, and, more significantly, Sorel's face was always there before me. Sorel loitering at the corner of her husband's eye like some irritating grit; Sorel staring upwards, mooning underneath *The Devil of Despair*; Sorel waiting in the bedroom of their East Melbourne house, all of course as Christopher must have seen her.

I was happy with the finished work. There was a sense of closure whilst giving the impression of ongoingness. My major regret being that the work would languish finally under another's name, especially given the numerous passages which were entirely from my own hand. In particular I might mention the final trilogy of letters, which I must confess excited me. I shall never forget those times in my study, seated before the blank page, wondering what exquisite perversity (still tenuously held within the bounds of literature) might be invented. Because I had no wish to merely reproduce the gross descriptions that accompanied the photos in my box of pornographic magazines, as I had with Avery's consideration of the young girl and the double penetration.

Why not, you ask, when the opportunity presented itself, simply give her Frances's letters and the journal with his incriminating dotings? Don't think this was not considered. But my very possession of these objects argued a complicity, and there was the problem too of my address upon the occasional aerogramme she chose to send. Too difficult.

You must understand that his relationship with Sorel, had to be discredited entirely: I could ill afford to offer him the defence, albeit mute, of having seen the error of his ways.

No, the manuscript had the advantage of my apparent ignorance, though I would let her, should the occasion arise, and of course it did, chivvy out of me my deep suspicion of a factual base. I could deliver it, as if a favour, as I might a recently discovered tale by Balzac.

And you must not forget that Christopher was going to die. I could not be seen discrediting him in Sorel's eyes. 'Don't speak ill of the dead' is not a proverb for nothing!

But mainly this, and I keep coming back, again, again, to make the point: *he wanted to confess*. And death would strip him of the opportunity.

The documents themselves were sufficient to indicate what his intentions were: remember he had left the outlines of an unfinished novel (if more proof were needed, he had written this infant draft, whatever it might be called, in twenty-leaf account books!). For him of course there could be no ending, no novel to be finished; nothing, that is, that would not celebrate his own atrocious behaviour, his weaknesses, his procrastination, his timidity.

Indeed, these jottings never possessed the courage of true confession; they were more an exercise in despair, their passage to abandonment apparent from the start.

I redrafted and I finished it, following the work, as he should have followed it in life, to its natural conclusion, that it might be given at least the dignity of excess.

All that now remained was to draft a letter to Sorel (a fiction which I found to be most difficult to write) feigning a *naïveté* and suggesting that I publish the novella, which I knew too well she had never seen, as a special number of my magazine.

It had of course the desired effect. The phone rang as expected. O, happy sound of her voice expressing such confusion and such ignorance!

'What novella?' she was asking, and God knows how I restrained myself.

I told her I would drop it in the mail immediately – this was the Wednesday evening, on the twenty-third.

And so it was that I imagined her, removing his novella from its package. Sitting down to read. As *I* sat down to read it, start to finish, twice again; at first with Sorel's eyes, and then my own.

Looking back, it seemed my greatest labour had been in writing out those passages concerning Gillian, and embellishing that evident disgust. The sacrifice of having to articulate the extent of the revulsion that he must have felt for Sorel, as close as I might imagine it (knowing too, the pain that it would cause her), was almost unbearable.

You must imagine me, in my study, set at this appalling task; imagine the excruciation for one so devoted to be involved in this act of debasing her, the acute difficulty of using words of hate about someone I loved so much. And to have succeeded!

It is late afternoon. The time of low sun through glass. Shadows of lace curtains bathe the walls, shadow and half-shadow, overlays of light.

A silent iridescence seems to have pervaded everything. In the corners of the room, the glimmer of back-reflections in the shadow.

The objects that surround me seem swathed in veils. Or is it mist? The sudden scintillation of an ash-tray. Glass against the glass of this table top. The air shimmers. The light strikes the surface of this half-filled flute. Palettes of reflection quiver at the walls. Onto the other glass of paintings. Everything is enhaloed.

I shall prosper.